ROAD TRIP

A GLOCK GRANNIES COZY MYSTERY

SHANNON VANBERGEN

Fairfield Publishing

Cover Design by Tina Adams

CONTENTS

"HATTIE!" I pleaded. "Please don't do it!"

I felt a breeze blow through my hair. Somewhere below us, birds were chirping, completely unaware or uncaring of what was about to happen. "Hattie," I said firmly, using the voice my mother would use to scold me when I was a little girl. "This is ridiculous. You're not thinking this through. Please step away from the ledge, and we can talk about this."

Hattie turned and looked at me, a hint of mischievousness in her eyes. She smiled, and for a brief second I thought maybe she would listen to me. But then she turned and took a step forward. She was gone.

I wanted to reach out and grab her, but it was too late. A cackle filled the air below and echoed through the trees. My stomach twisted in knots as I heard her voice getting further and further away.

"Ma'am?" A man's voice brought my attention back to the ledge. "Are you ready?"

I looked at him, fear rising up in my stomach. No, I was not ready.

My fear was obvious, and he laughed. "Look, if those old ladies can do this, so can you. There's no way I'm letting you get out of this. You'll regret it for the rest of your life."

He clearly didn't know me.

I looked at the name tag that was pinned onto his bright green Sky Extreme Zip Lines T-shirt.

"Look, Shane, this is all a mistake. I was just up here to make sure the grannies made it up safely. Now that they're all okay and safely on the ground, I'll just climb back down the way I came up and be on my way."

He blocked me from the steps, which honestly looked even scarier than the zip line.

"You can't do that," he said, smiling. "There's only one way up and one way down. Besides, you're already strapped in the harness."

His walkie-talkie went off, and a muffled voice came from his hip, where he had it secured to his belt. "Is there a problem up there?"

Shane picked up his walkie-talkie and spoke. "No problem here. Just checking the harness, and then I'll send her down."

"Good," the voice said. "The next one I'm sending up is celebrating her tenth birthday, so maybe sing to her or something. You know, make it special."

Shane looked at me while he clipped his walkie-talkie back to his belt. "Ten years old. Did you hear that?"

I sighed. "Yes, I heard it. Just make sure this thing is on tight." I tugged at my harness to see if it felt snug.

Shane looked it over. "You're all set! Are you ready?"

I took a deep breath and stood on the edge. I wasn't even close to being ready, but the grannies would never let me live it down if I didn't do this. And even though I thought I could live with that, for some reason, I didn't want to look like a wimp in front of Shane.

I held onto the rope that hung in front of my face, the only thing that would keep me from plunging to my death, said a quick prayer, and stepped off.

As soon as I was dangling in the air, my fear was replaced with adrenaline. I zipped through the trees, laughing and screaming. The view was amazing. Everything was so green in Missouri. I took in a breath as the air whooshed past my face. The woodsy smell made me smile and feel calm, even that high up and flying through the air at forty miles per hour (a fun fact that Shane had shared before the grannies made their jump). All too soon, the platform came into view, and my ride was nearly over. As I planted my feet on the wooden decking, the grannies cheered. I had done it and lived to tell the tale.

Back in Virginia's SUV, I pulled a souvenir T-shirt out of a bag from the gift shop and held it up, admiring it. It had the same design as Shane's, but the T-shirt was yellow.

"Hand me mine," Hattie said from the middle row. I pulled out a pink shirt and handed it up to her.

From the front seat, Greta laughed. "I can't believe we all did that!"

"I can't believe *Nikki* did that," Irene scoffed. "You act older than we are! Hand me my shirt. I got the red one."

I fished out her shirt. "Anybody else want theirs?"

"No, but I'd like a piece of that salted caramel we bought." Virginia reached her hand back and a piece was passed up to her. I grabbed a few for myself and threw them in my purse.

Minutes later, we were back on the road, Virginia driving us to Branson, Missouri. I looked out the window as the rock formations flew by. Missouri was a beautiful state. It had taken us two days to get this far, and you'd think riding in a vehicle that long with five grannies would make for a pretty boring trip, but it had been anything but. We had laughed, shared stories, even cried a few times. As I looked around the SUV, Virginia driving with Greta by her side, Hattie and Irene in the middle row, and Grandma Dean and me in the back, I knew this was a trip I would cherish for the rest of my life.

Greta turned around and waved her notebook in her hand. "We'll be there in about forty-five minutes!

That gives us enough time to answer a few more questions if you want!"

Those "questions" are what had kept us busy for the last two days. Greta had made a list of things to ask us —some funny and some serious. It was fun to get to know the grannies this way. Information that never would've come out before was suddenly told in great detail. We had all learned a lot about each other. The grannies, who had known each other for years, were often surprised at some of their answers.

"Only if you have more of that pineapple upside-down cake," Irene answered.

Greta smiled and turned around. I could hear her shuffling things in her bag. Soon, she was facing us again and handing out little plastic containers and forks. That was one thing you could always count on with the grannies—they had more food stored in their purses than most people did in their pantries.

I opened my container and was hit with the cheerful smell of pineapple. Greta made the best cakes, pies, and cookies, and lucky for us, she had brought plenty of treats for our trip.

As we sunk our forks into the sweet, moist cake, Greta read the first question. "Okay, what is the weirdest smell you've ever smelled?"

"Lloyd," I blurted out. The grannies laughed. Lloyd was the resident ladies' man at the retirement home where the grannies lived and where I stayed with

Grandma Dean. For some reason, he frequently smelled like hotdogs.

Hattie chuckled. "He's my Oscar Mayer wiener." Hattie and Lloyd were dating and, most likely, soon-to-be engaged. The man never wore anything more than a Speedo and a robe, and his new nickname was now etched in my mind and would haunt me forever. Thanks a lot, Hattie.

Irene spoke up. "Hattie, do you remember that one time we went fishing, and when we were packing up, I put the container of bait in the cooler with our lunch leftovers?"

Hattie made a face. "Oh yeah, and the pickles tipped over somehow."

"And then we left it in your car for a week," Irene finished.

"Please tell me you threw it all away and didn't even open the cooler," Grandma said, cringing.

"Oh, we opened it," Hattie said. "And then we nearly died."

"That was the strangest smell," Irene added. "The bait, our left-over egg sandwiches, and the pickle juice, all rotting in the Florida heat for a week."

Hattie laughed. "And then we put it on my kitchen counter, and Lloyd came in and asked what smelled so good, and he ate the pickles!"

I gagged. "Didn't you try to stop him?!"

Hattie shrugged. "It wouldn't have done any good. That man has never seen a pickle he didn't like."

"Next question," Virginia said as she drove.

"Okay, let me see . . ." Greta scanned the page, and then she said, "Here's a good one! What is something you had to learn the hard way?"

"I've got one," Hattie said. "Don't take a sleeping pill and a laxative the same night. I'll just tell you right now that doesn't end well."

The grannies chuckled, and then Virginia spoke up. "If someone is upset, don't ask them if it's because of their haircut. My sister didn't talk to me for weeks after that one."

I looked over at Grandma Dean and noticed that she was quietly looking out the window. I glanced up at the grannies and could tell they all saw the same thing. Greta gave me a reassuring smile, then turned around in her seat. The SUV was quiet.

I could only imagine what Grandma Dean was thinking. She was the whole reason we were making this trip. Many years ago, she had been married to the man of her dreams, a man named Thomas, the mother of her unborn baby. Her mother-in-law had made them get an annulment—all because she didn't think Grandma Dean was good enough for her son.

Grandma spent the next several years trying to prove her worth. She tried to get in touch with Thomas to tell him she was pregnant, but his mother refused every letter that was sent. Thankfully, Grandma Dean met Glenn. First he was her agent, and then he became her husband. By then, Grandma Dean was famous in

Europe for her commercials, her part in a soap opera, and later, movies. She was a singer, dancer, actress—and she was amazing at all of them.

And now here she was, early seventies, riding to Branson, Missouri to finally come face-to-face with the man that had been ripped from her a little over a half century ago. I didn't even know what would be going through my mind if I were her.

Thomas didn't know we were coming. Virginia had done a Google search and found his address. That was a week ago. Now here we were, passing a sign that said Branson was just thirty-two miles away.

I reached over and put my hand on hers and gave it a little squeeze. She squeezed back, but didn't take her eyes off the window.

We were quiet the rest of the way, not knowing what we could uncover on this road trip, but knowing that for Grandma Dean, it could be life changing.

2

I STEPPED out of the SUV and stretched. It felt so good to be out of the vehicle. We grabbed our suitcases from the back and headed to the hotel's front door. The quietness from the last few miles of the trip was slowly being replaced by the excitement of finally arriving.

Virginia opened the door of the hotel, and we all walked in. It wasn't a new or modern place. Instead, it was cozy and charming. It had a lived-in look that welcomed you right in.

The woman behind the desk greeted us with a big smile. "Welcome! I'm Paulette! What can I do for you?"

Grandma told her we had reservations, and while she checked us in, I walked around the lobby. There was a small coffee area in the corner, a glass coffee table surrounded by a few chairs, and toward the back of the lobby, a couch. Even though I had sat for hours on end, I wanted to flop down and rest. Why was traveling so exhausting?

"Isn't this adorable!" Greta said, picking up a couch pillow that had colorful birds embroidered on it. "I've always admired people who could do this."

"What's out here?" Virginia asked, already opening a door that led outside. "Oh look, girls! It's a little patio!"

We walked outside, and Hattie practically skipped down the few steps that led off the patio on the other side. "A koi pond!" she shrieked.

We joined Hattie and watched the bright orange fish as they swam up to us, realized we weren't going to feed them, and swam away. "This is making me hungry," Hattie said. "I wonder if we can get a good fish dinner around here somewhere. Let's go back inside and ask Paulette where we should eat!"

My stomach grumbled, so I followed Hattie inside, the other grannies right behind me. Grandma was just finishing up when we walked in.

"Hey, Paulette," Hattie called out. "Where's a good place to eat?"

Paulette grabbed a piece a of paper. "I'll jot down a few restaurants for you. We have a lot of good ones!"

She handed Grandma the paper, and we thanked Paulette and followed Grandma out the door. It was the kind of hotel where the rooms were all accessible from the outside, so Grandma gave the grannies their keys and room numbers. Instead of taking our luggage and heading to our rooms, we all stood there staring at Grandma Dean.

"Why are you all looking at me like that?" she asked.

We glanced at each other. Who was going to bring it up? Virginia decided to be the brave one. "Are we heading over to see Thomas tonight? Maybe after dinner?"

Grandma shook her head. "I'm too worn out. Let's give it a day or two." She looked down at the list from Paulette. "There's a pizza place on here. You ladies want to give that a try?"

"I think Hattie was hoping for fish," I pointed out.

Hattie shook her head. "Nah, it just sounded good while we were looking at the koi pond. I'm okay with pizza."

"Let's freshen up and meet out here in half an hour," Grandma said, grabbing the handle of her suitcase.

We divided into pairs and walked to our rooms. "Hattie is so strange. She's the only person I know who can stare at a koi pond and suddenly crave fish."

Grandma laughed. "You think that's bad? One time I went with her to a western store so she could buy herself a cowboy hat and boots for some line dancing class she and Irene were taking. We had to leave before she even bought anything because she said the smell of leather made her want to eat steak. It was so intense, she ended up having to order a hat and boots made out of vegan leather off the internet."

"Vegan leather?" I laughed. "What the heck is that?"

11

"I have no idea," Grandma said, rolling her eyes.

Our room was just as homey as the lobby had been. Grandma washed her face and reapplied her makeup, brushed her hair, and changed her clothes. She looked over at me and grimaced. "Aren't you going to freshen up?"

"I sprayed myself with some body spray," I said from my chair in the corner.

Grandma sniffed the air. "Why does it smell like Lysol in here? It didn't smell like that when we first walked in."

"Fine. I sprayed myself with Lysol," I admitted. I forgot to bring body spray, but thankfully, I found a little can of Lysol in my luggage. I had no idea how long it had been in there, but I figured it was better than nothing.

"Please tell me you're joking," Grandma said walking over to me and grabbing the can off the nightstand. "Crisp linen? Really, Nikki, this is your way of freshening up?"

"Hey, I smell better than I did before, and ninety-nine percent of my bacteria is now gone."

Grandma rolled her eyes. "If Kitty Purry were here . . ."

Kitty Purry was one of Grandma's cats. The other was Catalie Portman. Kitty was a diva and the one that Grandma consulted when she was doing my hair or makeup, and apparently, about my choice in body sprays.

Grandma put the can down. "Come on," she said pulling me to the bathroom. "Let's do . . . something with you."

I was used to this routine. Grandma was always fixing me up. She had me wash my face and then put on the mandatory mascara and lip gloss. She stood back and smiled.

"There! That really livened you up!" She was right. My eyes looked brighter, and I looked more awake . . . and somehow, I felt more awake. Maybe there was something to this "freshening up" thing after all.

Ten minutes later, we were all piling in Virginia's SUV and putting on our seat belts. Once all the doors closed, Hattie sniffed the air. "Why does it smell like someone threw up in here, then doused the car with Lysol?"

All the grannies sniffed. "It's Nikki," Grandma finally said. All eyes were on me for a moment.

"It figures," Irene said, turning around in her seat.

I had learned a lot about older people in the months I had lived with Grandma. They could be extremely caring and encouraging . . . they could also be brutally honest, their filters having disintegrated along with their collagen.

But I knew they loved me, and they meant well. I also knew this would be the last time I would use Lysol as a body spray.

As soon as we walked into the restaurant, the smell of pizza made my stomach rumble. There was a buffet

SHANNON VANBERGEN

with just about every kind of pizza you could imagine. I couldn't wait to get my plate and pile it high. And that's just what I did, adding a little bit of a salad on the side so I wouldn't get a lecture from the grannies about eating more vegetables.

We were sitting at the table eating and looking over some Branson brochures we had picked up in the hotel lobby when a woman approached our table and startled us. She smiled and moved her blond hair out of her face.

"I'm sorry to bother you ladies, but I wanted to invite you to my show later tonight." She put a flyer in the middle of the table. "My name is Crystal Star." She paused, and her cheeks blushed a little. "Well, my real name is Amy Walters but that sounded boring, so I gave myself a stage name. I have no idea why I just told you that."

Grandma put her hand on Crystal's . . . or Amy's . . . arm. "Amy is a beautiful name, and you picked out a wonderful stage name. But if you're going to be Crystal, you have to own it. If you don't believe it, others won't either."

The girl smiled and seemed to relax a little. "I'm just getting started here in the Branson area. I would do anything to be a big star. It's been my dream since I was a little girl. I'd love to see you ladies in the audience. I'm playing all weekend."

Grandma looked at the flyer and then back up at her, surprised. "Your show starts at six o'clock. That's

14

in one hour! Shouldn't you be at the theater getting ready?"

Amy blushed again. "Well, if I don't get an audience together, there won't be a show."

Grandma nodded and smiled. "We'll be there."

Amy's face lit up. "Thank you so much! I'll see you ladies soon!"

"Wait!" Greta called after her. Amy came back to our table. "Why don't you leave those flyers with us? We'll hand them out here in the restaurant for you."

"Really?" Amy asked, surprised. "You would do that for me?"

"Of course," Grandma added. "Now get to that theater. You're making me nervous with how close you're cutting it."

Amy laughed and thanked the grannies, then she ran out of the restaurant. Greta held the stack of flyers in her hand. "Poor girl, I hope she can make it out here. I imagine it's pretty cutthroat."

Before Greta could say anything else, another woman walked up to our table. She also had a stack of flyers in her hand, but she was completely different than Amy. This woman was confident as she slapped her flyer on the table. "You ladies look like you're in the mood for some real southern fun!" Her accent and big smile immediately had us hooked. Her auburn hair was lightly curled as it hung down over her flannel-covered shoulders. She tipped her cowboy hat to us, and her blue eyes seemed to sparkle. "My name is Madison

15

Paige," she pointed to her professional looking flyer, a big upgrade from Amy's simple, printed page. "I sing all the classic country songs, but I especially love anything by Barbara Mandrell."

"Oh, I just love her," Greta crooned.

"Well then, you'll love me!" Madison declared. "I've got a show tomorrow and Sunday afternoon!"

I wasn't a fan of country music, but her southern accent and charismatic personality made me want to go see her show anyway.

Grandma looked up at her. "You don't seem like the kind of person who would need to go to restaurants to get a following."

Madison laughed. "It's hard to get started in this town. Thankfully, I have a lot of fans already. But you can never have too many! Will I see you this weekend?"

"We'll be there!" Greta assured her.

Madison flashed her winning smile, clicked her cowboy boots together, and tipped her hat. "Great! I'll see you then!"

As she walked away, Grandma looked over at us. "Let's eat and get out of here before we agree to any more shows."

"Good idea," Hattie said. "And now I'm hungry for steak . . . and for some reason, peach cobbler."

3

WE ATE AS QUICKLY as we could, handed out Amy's flyers, and then made our way to the theater.

"This can't be right," Virginia said as she pulled into the parking lot. Overgrown grass waved in the breeze next to a building that looked like it had once been a restaurant.

"This is the address," Greta assured her, though she didn't really sound that sure herself.

We sat in the car a few minutes until Grandma unbuckled her seat belt. "Well, let's go check it out."

As we walked up to the door, I couldn't help but notice we were the only car in the parking lot. I got an uneasy feeling in my stomach. "You don't think this is some sort of setup, do you? We're not going to walk in and be ambushed . . . right?"

Irene looked back at me. "Honestly, Nikki. You and

your imagination. We're twenty minutes early. I'm sure someone else will show up.

Sadly, no one did. We were the only ones sitting on the folding chairs in front of a makeshift stage. But Amy Walters, well, Crystal Star, sang her heart out. When it was over, she stepped off the stage to talk to us.

"You have the voice of an angel!" Greta said, shaking her hand.

"Aw, thank you," Amy answered, her cheeks blushing a little. "Thank you so much for coming."

"Do you have any more of those flyers?" Grandma Dean asked her. "We'd be happy to hand them out as we explore Branson. Everyone needs to hear your voice."

Amy looked excited. "I do, actually! I'll go get them!"

She disappeared through a door, and we watched the three guys in the band pack up their instruments. They didn't seem very happy. One of them started bickering with another, but they managed to talk quietly enough so I couldn't understand what they were saying.

Amy came out carrying a leather computer bag, and when she got near, she noticed we were watching the argument unfold in front of us.

"Pay no attention to them," she said handing Grandma a stack of flyers. "It's been stressful lately. We've tried and tried to get people in here, but we haven't had any luck. Last night, no one showed up at all."

Grandma patted her on the shoulder. "We'll see what we can do. Maybe we can get a few more people in here."

"You really should have a sign out front," Virginia told her. "We didn't even know we were in the right place."

Amy sighed. "We can't afford one. I made one out of poster board, but it keeps blowing away."

As we walked to the parking lot, Grandma Dean looked somber.

"Are you okay?" I asked her.

"I just feel bad for that girl. I know what it's like to struggle to make your dreams come true."

"Yeah," I said. "But you didn't give up, and you made it. She just needs to put in some more time, work a little harder, not give up, right?"

Grandma shrugged. "Sometimes I wonder if I made it because of my talent or because I married a really good agent."

Grandma's words hit me hard. I didn't realize after all these years she was still questioning herself. I put my arm around her. "You made it because you were really talented, *and* you had a great agent. You and Grandpa Dean were a good team."

That made Grandma smile. "That we were."

As we drove out of the parking lot, Greta turned

19

back to look at us. "So, what now? It's only seven o'clock. It seems too early to go back to the hotel."

"We could see another show," Virginia suggested. "Surely there's something else happening tonight."

We drove down the strip and passed billboard after billboard. There was a show for everything—country, fifties music, comedians, acrobats, musicals.

"Look at that one!" Irene said pointing out her window. "That's the fifth time I've seen that since we turned onto this road. Let's see if he has a show tonight."

I looked out my window and saw the big sign for Archer Nash—Branson's hottest show. Of course, all the billboards said that, so who knew how great he really was.

Greta grabbed her phone. "I'll look him up!" She typed in a few things, then looked back at us. "He has a show at eight, and we can still get tickets! We have time to make it!"

"Let's do it!" we all yelled.

Even though I had no idea what to expect, I had a feeling we were going to see what a true Branson show was really about.

4

"THIS IS SO FUN!" Virginia said, looking around the large, round two-story room. And that's what it was, a room. There was a round stage in the center that was surrounded by rows and rows of seats. Upstairs, there were more seats and a bar area. We were among the first people in, so we grabbed a seat in the front row. Of course, this wasn't the main show, this was just the preshow. A group called Willie, Billie, and Lou would be performing any minute, getting the crowd ready for the main attraction, Archer Nash. At that point, we would be ushered into the theater and would sit in our assigned seats.

"Let's go grab some drinks!" Irene said, standing. "What do you gals want?"

"A Diet Coke for me," Greta answered.

"Can you see if they have coffee?" Virginia asked.

Irene rolled her eyes. "We're not sitting in a cafe

back home. We're in Branson, Missouri! We're going to live it up!"

She and Hattie got up to get drinks, and I had no idea what they would come back with, but I was sure whatever it was would cause me to have a headache in the morning.

Sure enough, they came back with colorful drinks in tall plastic cups that had Archer Nash's name splashed across the front. Irene started handing them out. "They were a bit weak, so we added a little somethin' somethin' from Hattie's purse."

That concerned me. A little "somethin' somethin'" from Hattie's purse could be anything from alcohol to that nasty liquid sour candy Hattie liked to pick up in the grocery store checkout line. I wasn't sure which one I hoped it was. One sip, though, and it was obvious. It wasn't sour.

"Good grief, Irene," Grandma said, pulling her drink away from her face. "Did you put gasoline in here?"

Irene laughed. "No, but close."

Hattie and Irene sat down, and Irene flipped open the program that listed the guys in the group and their biographies. "I have dibs on Willie!" she said matter-of-factly.

Greta looked over at her. "Why do you get dibs?"

"Oh," she said apologetically, "did you call it first?"

Greta blushed. "No! I meant . . ."

She didn't get to finish because Hattie spoke up.

"That's not fair! You sat down before I did and opened the program before I could. I want Willie! You can have Billie or Lou."

"Girls," Grandma said in a hushed yell, "people can hear you."

"Good," Irene answered. "Then they'll all hear that I have dibs on Willie."

Virginia took a sip of her drink and made a face. "You don't even know what he's like. He could be a terrible person."

Irene laughed. "I don't care what kind of person he is. He plays the harmonica."

"What's so great about that?" I asked. As soon as I said it, Hattie and Irene smiled wildly, and the other grannies groaned. I didn't know how Irene would answer, but I knew it would make me regret asking.

"Any man who can do that with his mouth is a man good enough for me. At least for one night."

"Irene!" Grandma said, not even bothering to keep her voice down. "You are so vulgar. One of these days, that is going to come back and bite you."

Irene's smiled. "Let's hope!"

I slunk down into my chair, my stomach feeling sick from either the turpentine Irene put in my drink or from the visual I just had of Irene and poor Willie.

Just then, colorful lights started flashing as the house lights dimmed. Three men in overalls jumped on the stage. One had a banjo, one a guitar, and one a harmonica.

"Welcome, folks!" they rang out, and the large crowd cheered.

The man with the guitar came to the front and spoke. "I'm Billie, and this here's my brother Willie." The man with the harmonica smiled and waved. "And this is our brother Lou." Lou played a fast-paced ditty on his banjo, and we all clapped along.

The crowd continued to laugh and clap their way through their act, and the few kids in the crowd loved their bluegrass rendition of "Baby Shark."

Then Willie pulled a fiddle out of a case and wowed us all with his talent as we clapped along to "Cotton-Eyed Joe." After the applause, he addressed the audience.

"We've been singin' together since we were little tots, and for the last twenty-five years, we've been doin' shows all over the country together. But no place is as great as Branson." We all cheered, and there were several whistles from people in the crowd. "Hopefully, y'all are having fun on your vacation. There's so much to see and do here."

Billie stepped forward, smiling. "Tell 'em what you did last week, Willie."

"Well," Willie said, "I decided to go see a few shows myself, so I went to see the great Russian Comedian on the strip."

"Was he funny?" Billie asked, setting him up for his joke.

"I don't know. I couldn't understand a single thing

he said. He was talkin' too fast. Everything he said he was rushin'." He looked at his brother. "Get it, he was rushin' . . . Russian."

Lou played a funny little song on his banjo, and the crowd groaned and laughed at Willie's bad joke. Greta thought it was hilarious and erupted into a laughter I had never heard from her. She caught Willie's eye, and he looked down and winked at her. To our surprise, Greta winked right back. I looked over at Irene, and she looked back at me, her mouth open in shock.

"Did Greta just flirt with him?" she mouthed. All I could do was shrug. I wasn't sure what was happening.

Throughout the forty-five-minute show, Willie looked over at Greta several times, and I caught them smiling at each other. When the show ended, she was beaming. "I can't imagine Archer Nash being any better than these guys. That show was great!"

I wanted to ask her about all the little smiles between her and Willie, but before I had a chance, a man walked over to us and tapped Greta on the shoulder.

"Excuse me, miss," he said as Greta turned to face him. "I was asked to give you this." He handed her a stack of cards with lanyards. "Willie asked me to give these to your group."

"What are they?" Greta asked, taking them.

"They are backstage passes. Once the Archer Nash show is over, meet me by the stage with these, and I'll take you back to meet the guys."

He walked away, and we all stood there in shock. Greta turned around, the cards dangling from her hand. "This doesn't mean they want us to do drugs with them, does it? I've seen that MTV show. I know what those rock stars do backstage."

Grandma chuckled and took a lanyard and put it around her neck. "I have a feeling the only drugs those guys are on are for high blood pressure and cholesterol."

"And maybe Viagra," Irene said with a wink.

Greta grew flustered. "I don't want anything to do with that either!"

Irene laughed, reaching over and taking her own lanyard. "Don't worry, Greta. I'm sure your virginity is safe tonight."

Greta looked hurt. "I'm not trying to be a prude. I just don't want them to expect anything for this."

I patted her on the shoulder. "Don't worry, Greta. We'll watch out for you."

"No offense, Nikki, but between you and loose lips and loose hips over there," she pointed to Hattie and Irene, "I'd rather have someone else watch out for me."

Hattie cackled. "Loose lips and loose hips! Which one am I?"

"Come on," Grandma said, passing me and Virginia our backstage passes. "Let's take our seats." She looked at Greta. "I'll make sure nothing happens to any of us."

Greta took a breath, and the tension eased from her shoulders. We made our way to our seats in the large theater. The place definitely looked like a concert hall. The stage was huge, and the instruments were all set up. Lights were everywhere, and the speakers looked enormous.

We didn't have great seats, but they weren't bad either. We hadn't been seated too long when the doors closed and the lights turned off, engulfing the theater in darkness. A purple glow shone on stage, and we all watched it in anticipation. The crowd was silent except for the occasional cough.

Where was Archer Nash? Then I saw movement. Coming down from the ceiling above the stage was a man dressed in all black, holding a guitar. The crowd went wild as the sound of an acoustic guitar filled the theater. And then we heard his voice. So deep that it rumbled through me and gave me goose bumps. It was almost haunting. It was a slow song I had never heard before, but the grannies must have known it because each one clutched her chest, and I heard Virginia sigh and say that she loved that song.

When the song was over, the applause was deafening. The stage lights came on, and I got a good look at Archer Nash. For a man in his mid to late sixties, he was very attractive. He looked fit, and his white hair made his tan skin look darker than it probably was. The grannies were mesmerized.

He took a sip of water as the band walked onto the stage. They started playing, and the crowd must have recognized the song, because they started cheering.

Once Archer Nash started singing, I recognized it too. It was a Willie Nelson song.

Two hours later, Archer Nash took a bow and walked off stage. We stood up to stretch, and Virginia fanned herself. "Whoo whee! He is a hottie! And that man can entertain!"

The other grannies agreed.

"Come on!" Greta said, reaching up and grabbing at the card that hung around her neck. "Let's go meet the guys!"

"I thought you were worried about that!" Irene said, picking up her purse.

"I've had two hours to get over it," Greta said, smiling.

We made our way to the stage, and sure enough, the man that had handed us the passes was standing there waiting for us. He ushered us backstage, and I felt like we were in the way. There was a flurry of activity as men and women were clearing the stage, and a large security team clogged the hall. Once we were finally past them, the man led us down one hall and to another.

"Their dressing rooms are right down here," he said, but then he stopped. I looked around him and could see a group of security guards standing at the end of the hall, and they didn't look happy.

"What's going on?" the man called to the team as he started walking again, quickening his pace. We all followed him, not sure what else to do. When we got to the door, we heard the word "body," and I glanced into the room. I immediately closed my eyes, wishing I hadn't just seen what was on the floor in the dressing room. I spun around, not wanting to face what was right before me, and saw the grannies, horror on their faces and hands clasped over their mouths. So much for a fun night on the town.

5

LOU WAS ON THE GROUND. And judging from the looks on the security team's faces, I knew he wouldn't be playing the banjo any longer.

Hattie and Irene pushed their way into the room to get a better look. "Yep," Hattie said walking back to the hallway. "He's dead as a door nail. There's nothing we can do to save him. Let's go get some peach cobbler."

The next few minutes were a blur, and I only caught bits and pieces of conversations around me. I heard that the police had been called, and Willie and Billie weren't in their dressing rooms. The grannies and I huddled in the hall, far enough away that we weren't in the way but close enough that we could hear what was going on.

Then up walked Billie and Willie with Archer Nash right behind them. Judging from the looks on their faces, someone had already told them about Lou. As

Willie walked by us, he stopped and gave Greta a small, sad smile. He reached up and gently squeezed her elbow. "I'm so sorry about this," he whispered.

"It's okay," she whispered. "We should leave."

He shook his head. "No, please don't. Can you ladies stick around?"

We all nodded our heads yes. Honestly, I didn't know if we could find our way out if we were asked to leave. I tried to picture the way we came through the halls, but my mind couldn't shake the image of Lou.

Willie and Billie, followed by Archer Nash, disappeared into Lou's dressing room. A few minutes later, Archer Nash came out by himself, rubbing his face and looking shook up. He talked in hushed tones to the security team for a minute, then walked over to us.

"Are you okay?" Grandma asked.

He looked up at us, truly seeing us for the first time, and he looked surprised that we were there. "Are you friends of Lou's?" he asked. And then he noticed our backstage passes.

"I'm so sorry," he said to us. "This is not the backstage experience we want our fans to have."

Greta spoke up. "Willie asked us to stay. Is that okay?"

He nodded and closed his eyes. He rubbed his face again, but didn't say anything. We stood there silently until we heard a commotion at the other end of the hall. It was the police.

Within minutes, they ushered everyone out of the room, and those of us lingering in the hall were brought back to the large theater. We were each questioned and given the business card of the detective we could call if we thought of any details that might help the case.

"Maybe we should just leave," Grandma said, pulling her purse over her shoulder. "I feel like we're in the way. And who knows how long the police will keep the guys here tonight."

Greta agreed, and we turned to walk away. Then we heard someone yelling for us to wait. It was Willie, and he was running down the aisle to catch up to us. He looked over at Greta. "I know this has been a crazy night, but I'd really like to get to know you a little better. I felt like we had some kind of . . . connection."

Greta reached out and took his hand. "We can meet some other time. I can give you my number . . ."

"We always meet at a little diner after each show. We're headed there as soon as the police say we can leave. I know it's late, but I'd really like it if you could meet us there." He looked up at the rest of us. "All of you."

"Well," Greta paused. "If you're up for it . . ."

"Thank you," he said. "I know this is not the night you hoped for, and I just met you and shouldn't lean on you, but . . . I feel like I need to be around you."

Greta blushed. Actually, I think we all did.

He gave us the address and told us to head to the diner, and he and the others would join us soon.

Silently, we made our way outside. Once in the vehicle, Virginia typed the address into her GPS.

Irene shifted in her seat. "No offense, Greta, but I can't believe that guy is that into you."

Greta turned to look at us. "No offense taken. I can't believe it either."

As she turned around, I noticed the hint of a smile. Greta was finally being noticed by a man, and she loved it.

We sat in the diner for about twenty minutes before the men came in. Willie looked relieved to see Greta, and he took a seat next to her. Archer Nash took a seat next to Grandma, who was at the head of the table. Billie sat across from us.

"I hope it's okay," Billie said to us. "We invited some other people here tonight. I thought we could all have a root beer float in honor of Lou. That's what he ordered every night we came here."

Our waitress came over and hugged each of the guys as she wiped a tear from her face. "I just can't believe this happened," she said to Billie. "Did he have a heart attack?"

Billie told her they didn't have any answers yet, but something in his expression told me he at least had an idea. I glanced at the grannies, and I could tell they noticed it too.

Soon, more people were coming into the diner and hugging Billie and Willie, then patting Archer Nash on the back to console him too.

I looked around at the table full of interesting characters, and that's exactly what they seemed like to me, characters. Billie must have watched me take in each one, because he stood up and introduced everyone, holding in his right hand the root beer float the waitress had just brought to him.

He pointed to a big, burly man with a short beard and an eyepatch. His red-and-black flannel shirt fit tightly across his broad chest, and he looked like a lumberjack. "This here is the Kodiak King. A big man with an even bigger heart. I know you and Lou had your differences, but he could always count on you." The man nodded in agreement, and Billie moved on to the next person at the table.

"Roxy Rococo," Billie smiled, and she smiled back. Her black hair and dark makeup made her look just like Joan Jett. "You always keep life interesting. You've been a friend to all of us for years, and I know Lou had a soft spot for you, even if you did always turn him down."

The men chuckled, and I noticed Archer Nash looked uncomfortable for a moment, but he quickly regained his composure when he saw that I was looking at him.

And then Billie looked over at a man that hadn't yet spoken a word. There was something about him that was . . . strange. He wore a black turtleneck even though it had been a very warm day. He seemed quiet and solemn, and I had a feeling it was more from his personality than the tragedy of the night. His dark eyes focused on Billie, and I noticed that his features seemed to be perfectly sculpted. He looked like a very attractive but very troubled man.

Billie stared him down, and his voice lowered. "And you, Casius Nine, are a deceptive thief and liar, and I have no idea why Lou was ever friends with you."

Well, that was an unexpected introduction. I saw Archer Nash wince, and the rest of the table was silent, all eyes on the mysterious man who simply looked at Billie with a grim smile and raised his glass. "To Lou," he said, "who loved us all."

"To Lou," the table repeated, and we all took a swig of our root beer floats.

An hour later, Grandma leaned over to me. "These men can really put away their root beer floats. I couldn't have another one if they paid me."

I was pretty sure I *could* have another one, but I kept quiet.

Billie ordered another round as Roxy Rococo told a funny story about Lou. "Remember how afraid he was of horses?" She stopped and laughed. "And we asked him one time why he was so afraid of them, and he said it was because when he was younger, he reached up and touched a neighbor's horse, and he felt its heartbeat, and for some reason, that freaked him out."

Billie laughed. "I don't understand why that had such an impact on him, but it did. He sure was talented, though. He was a natural with the banjo. He could play several instruments, and he learned them all by ear." Billie shook his head. "But boy, was he stubborn."

I could sense some animosity, but who hadn't felt that against a sibling from time to time?

The group of friends, all Branson performers, took turns telling their favorite stories. At times, we laughed so hard, we cried. It made me sad that I had never actually met the guy, just watched him in his last performance, making the crowd laugh and cheer as he played his banjo.

At two in the morning, Casius stood and said he was going to head home. Everyone said goodbye to him except for Billie. Once he was gone, the others stood up and said they were going to call it a night too. Willie gave them each a hug and talked to them for a minute. I assumed we were going to stick around so he and Greta could say their goodbyes, but instead Greta pulled out a little container from her purse and handed it to him before he finished talking to his friends. "I wish I could do something more to help you. But here's a piece of my pineapple upside-down cake."

He thanked her, and she walked out with us. It seemed strange that that was it.

"That was a weird goodbye," Virginia said to her on

the way to the parking lot. "Are you sure you don't want to stick around for a while? Maybe give him your number or something so you guys can get together again?"

Greta shrugged. "He's dealing with a lot right now. If he needs me, he can find me."

I had no idea how Willie would ever find Greta. I wasn't even sure she ever told him her last name. But I figured if that's how Greta wanted to play this, that was her choice.

That night, I couldn't sleep. The image of Lou sprawled out on the floor in his dressing room kept flashing in my mind. Billie knew something that he didn't share with the table. He suspected Lou's death wasn't an accident. I could feel it in my gut.

My mind started reeling with possibilities. I hadn't seen any blood on Lou. He was lying on his stomach, though, so there could have been a wound to his chest or neck I couldn't see. But if the wound was bad enough to kill him, wouldn't there be blood around him? He could've been strangled . . . I sighed. Unfortunately, I had learned in my several months with the grannies that there were many ways to murder someone.

I looked at the clock beside my bed. It felt like the red light of the numbers was searing into my tired eyes. Five thirty. I wanted to call Owen and tell him what had happened. He would be getting up for work soon—a detective like him was always up early, even when he had a day off. I could text him . . .

No, I told myself. We had left on strange terms. I didn't even get to see him before I left town. Just a few weeks ago, he had admitted he had feelings for me—but was planning on taking a job out of state, if it was offered to him. And when that fell through, well, it felt like he had only told me about his feelings because it felt safe when he thought he was moving away. But where did that leave us, now that he was staying? And now that I knew he was looking for another job outside of Florida, it felt like anything we could have together would be short-term.

What did I want? Did I want something long-term with Owen? I felt like I did when I was with him, but for some reason, being this far away, I felt . . . indifferent. And then I thought of Joe, the hunky fireman I had fallen for, and then completely screwed up any chance of having a relationship with after my fiancé from Illinois showed up and introduced himself.

I started to berate myself, then stopped. No, that was the old Nikki. The new Nikki was not boy crazy and didn't jump at every chance to be with a guy. I thought back to the diner when I had met the Kodiak King and that strange man, Casius Nine. Both had been close to my age, though I would guess that Casius was a bit older, maybe mid-thirties compared to my nearly thirty. Other than being intrigued by both of them, I didn't have any desire to chase after either one. Though

I never was a chaser. Guys usually came to me, and I just followed. Who knows, maybe if they had shown an interest in me, I would've reciprocated.

How could I be nearly thirty years old and still know so little about myself?

The last time I looked at the clock, it was nearly seven. As sunlight poured into the room, I finally fell asleep. Maybe it was because I felt safe now that it was daylight. Or maybe it was because my brain had finally worked its way through all of my worries. Either way, I was grateful for the rest.

I woke up a few hours later in a panic, not knowing where I was. I sat up and looked around. Oh, that's right, the charming little hotel in Branson. I looked over, and Grandma wasn't in the room, but I noticed a note sitting on her pillow.

Nikki, I'm having lunch with Archer Nash. Stop right there. Don't read more into this than there is. We're just having lunch. Maybe I can get some more information on what happened last night with Lou. If you have lunch with the others, please make sure Hattie and Irene stay out of trouble. You know how they can be.

Love, Geraldine

P.S. Owen called me this morning worried about you. He texted you several times this morning, and when you didn't reply, he called me. I explained that we had a fairly wild night last night, and you were sleeping in.

First, I laughed that she signed her named Geraldine and not Grandma. While most women held that title near and dear to their hearts, Grandma Dean despised it. She said it made her sound old. She always insisted I call her Gigi, Peaches, or Mimi, which I never did. And, instead of calling me her granddaughter, I was always introduced as "her daughter's daughter."

I walked over to my nightstand and picked up my phone. Sure enough, Owen had texted three times. I debated whether or not to call him back, but finally decided not to. Grandma told him I was fine, so he shouldn't be worrying anymore. Since it was nearly noon, I decided to text the other grannies and see what they were doing for lunch.

While I was getting ready, Irene texted me that they were in the lobby trying to figure out what to do. I told them I'd be right there.

Paulette was smiling when I walked in. "Your friends are on the patio," she said, pointing to the door across the lobby. I thanked her and walked outside. Irene and Hattie didn't look happy.

"What's going on?" I asked. "Where are Greta and Virginia?"

Irene let out a *humph*. "It looks like our little Greta is craftier than we thought." She handed me an empty plastic container, the kind Greta had stored pieces of pineapple upside-down cake in.

I took it, confused. "I don't understand. What does this have to do with anything?"

"That's the container Greta gave to Willie last night."

"How did she get it back? How in the world did he find her?"

Irene scoffed. "Flip it over."

When I did, I laughed. I had forgotten that Greta labeled all of her containers with her name and phone number. She handed out a lot of treats, and she always wanted her containers back. "Well, that sly dog," I said, looking over the label. "And here we thought she left without giving him her number."

Hattie had been looking at the koi pond and finally joined us on the patio. "Yeah, and Willie called her while we were out here waiting for you. He and Billie came by and picked her and Virginia up for a lunch date! Can you believe that! They stole our men!"

"Hattie," I said firmly. "You have a boyfriend. Let Greta and Virginia have some fun."

"Technically, Virginia has a boyfriend too," Hattie pointed out. "That secret guy she's dating . . . Hershel or something."

She was right. I had forgotten all about him. Virginia hadn't brought him up since Grandma and I first uncovered her secret a few weeks ago.

"Well, either way," I finally said. "They never get to be wild and free. Let them have this. I'm sure there is other trouble you two could get into."

As soon as I said it, I regretted it. Grandma had specifically said to make sure they didn't get into trouble, and here I was, encouraging it. Well, it backfired on me right away.

Hattie smiled and looked at Irene. "She's right! There are plenty of other performers here we can hang out with! Let's go find us some semi-famous men!"

Irene jumped out of her chair and dangled a set of keys. "Virginia left us her SUV! Let's go!"

I followed them to the lobby, and Irene turned and looked at me. "Where are you going?"

"Umm, with you. To get some lunch and find some semi-famous men."

"Oh no, you don't have what it takes to hang out with Hattie and me. You couldn't handle it. You would just slow us down with your guilt."

I started to object, but knew she was right. So I stood there and watched them walk out to the parking lot. As they left, I heard Hattie make a suggestion for lunch. "Let's go grab a fish dinner somewhere. Those koi are really giving me a hankering for some fish.

I looked up at Paulette, helpless and alone.

"You could always call an Uber," she suggested. "You might even get one of our performers. Sometimes they drive to make extra money. Then you can explore Branson a little on your own."

She was being so nice, but the last thing I wanted to do was to explore Branson by myself. I decided to walk across the street to the gas station to get a Mountain Dew and a Snickers bar. While I was waiting in line, I was surprised to hear my name. I turned around and saw Casius Nine standing behind me with a coffee cup in one hand and a protein bar in the other.

"Nikki, right?" he said, furrowing his brows like he wasn't so sure.

He was wearing a suit and a bolo hat and didn't look quite as ominous as he had the night before, though he did look very well dressed. "Yes," I answered. "And you're the mysterious Casius Nine."

He chuckled. "What are you doing here, other than giving yourself diabetes?" He pointed to my lunch choices.

I sighed. "My friends abandoned me. But it's not all bad. This candy bar has . . ." I checked the wrapper, "four whole grams of protein."

"Oh, well then," he laughed. "I'm glad you're taken care of."

I turned back around. Why was my heart pounding? That's usually how it felt *after* I consumed a bottle of Mountain Dew and ate a candy bar, not before it.

After paying for my not-so-healthy lunch, I started to leave, but Casius called my name again. "Wait up." He signed a credit card receipt and then made his way to the door where I was standing. "You know, I could always run you somewhere for lunch. I have to make a quick stop first, but then I can take you anywhere you want."

His introduction from the night before sent a cold shiver up my spine. "I usually don't get in the car with . . . what did Billie call you . . . a thief and a liar." I ended the sentence with a smile, you know, so he wouldn't take offense and kill me or something.

But if I offended him, he didn't show it. "Well, what kind of magician would I be if I wasn't a thief and a liar?"

"You're a magician?" I asked, though now that I looked at him, he definitely fit the part. After the introductions from the night before, I knew that the Kodiak King did animal shows, and Roxy Rococo was indeed a Joan Jett impersonator who also sang other songs from the eighties in her show. But no one had said what Casius Nine did, and he hadn't offered up any information the night before either.

I raised an eyebrow. "So, is that what Billie meant when he called you those things? That you were just a magician?" I asked.

"No," Casius said. "He truly meant I was a thief and a liar, though I think he's wrong on both counts."

Why did Casius have to be so darn charming? There was definitely something dark about him, but was he dangerous? I was tempted, really tempted, to get in the car with him. He could see my hesitation.

"I'll tell you what, I have to drop something off at my theater, and then I'll grab us both lunch and bring it back to your hotel. Are you staying over there?" He pointed across the street, and I nodded. "I can see some outside tables from here. We'll eat outside, and you can be sure I won't murder you in public."

I thought it over for a moment.

"And there will be no lying or thievery either," he added.

That made me laugh. "Ok, fine. I'll wait outside for you."

"Great!" He smiled at me, and my heart did that thing it does when I drink my Mountain Dew too quickly. Only this time, I knew it wasn't caffeine induced.

As I walked across the street, I had to have a talk with myself. *Pull it together, Nikki! You are not going to fall for this guy. You can talk to him and make sure he isn't a suspect in case Lou was actually murdered.*

I sat out there for forty minutes, wondering if I was crazy, and then I saw him pull up. My heart raced. Should I text Grandma and let her know I was having lunch with Casius just in case I ended up missing? That suddenly sounded like a good idea. She responded right away. And her text sent another cold chill down my spine.

6

"BE CAREFUL. Lou was definitely murdered. Anyone could be his killer."

I read the text from Grandma twice and was shaking when Casius walked over and put the food on the table. He looked concerned. "You okay? You know, if you're not comfortable, I can just give you your food and leave. I don't have to stay."

I looked up at him. "No, I, uh . . . I just got a text that rattled me, that's all. But I'm fine."

The smell from the fast-food bags filled the air and redirected my thoughts. "After you made fun of my gas station snacks, I was afraid you were going to come back with tofu or something."

He winked. "I can tell you're more of a burger-and-fries kind of girl."

Should I be offended by that? No time, the burger and fries were getting cold.

He took the food out of the bag and sat down across from me. The burger smelled amazing, but you have to eat the fries while they're hot.

I glanced up at him. "Can you pass me a ketchup packet?"

He stretched out his arm, the ketchup packet in the palm of his hand. Just as I was about to grab it, he closed his fingers over it and waved his left hand over his fist. He opened his hand, and the ketchup packet was gone.

I burst into laughter. "That's awesome! But don't come between me and my food. Where's my ketchup?"

He reached over to my ear and smiled. When he pulled his hand back, he was holding the packet.

Ugh. Magicians. I guess they can't help themselves.

"So," I said, opening the packet, "how did you meet Lou?"

His smile faded. "In Vegas, actually. I was trying to make it out there about twelve years ago, and he was out there visiting friends. Somehow, we managed to sit down at a poker table together, and we just kind of . . . hit it off. We were fast friends, I guess you could say. He was old enough to be my dad, but he had this fun, childish way about him. We got a couple of drinks, and he told me if I couldn't make it in Vegas, I should go to Branson. Two months later, I got in my car with what little I had and headed out here. He helped me get established, get settled."

"But Billie doesn't like you, I take it?" I asked.

"Ha! Billie doesn't like a lot of people. But I don't blame him. He was overly protective of Lou. Lou had a heart condition since birth, and Billie always looked out for him." Casius was quiet for a minute. "I'm assuming that's why he died. Heart attack or something. I haven't heard if they've released his cause of death yet."

I didn't know how Grandma had heard the news, and until I had more details, I didn't want to tell Casius. My heart filled with sadness. I had thought maybe he had killed his friend, but now I was pretty sure he didn't.

"You all right there?" he said poking me in the shoulder. "You're pretty up and down."

I picked up my burger, trying to change the subject. "I think I just need some protein. That four grams from earlier didn't do much for me."

"You ate the candy bar anyway? Even when you knew I was bringing you food?" He laughed at me and shook his head. "You have zero self-control."

I pulled back the wrapper of my burger. "I'm not even going to pretend otherwise."

We sat outside and enjoyed the Branson sunshine while we ate our lunch. It wasn't as warm as the day before, and it felt nice to be outside. We sat there and talked for nearly two hours until he looked at his phone and grimaced. "I need to head to the theater. I have a show in a few hours, and I need to take care of some things."

He stood up and put our trash in the fast-food bag. "Maybe I can see you again sometime?" he asked. "Unless it would make your boyfriend jealous ..."

Casius was fishing for information. "I don't have a boyfriend," I answered honestly. "What about you?"

He smirked. "Nope, no boyfriend either."

I stood up next to him and lightly punched him in the arm. "You know what I mean."

"I know, I know. No, I don't have a girlfriend. It's hard to be an entertainer and find a girlfriend. Women come up to me after the show all the time, but they don't see me, they see my dark and dangerous persona. For some reason, chicks dig that."

I couldn't help but laugh.

"What? You don't think that's true?" he asked.

"Oh, I believe it," I answered. "I was just thinking about how you came across last night at the diner. I definitely thought you were dark and dangerous."

"And what do you think now?"

I thought for a minute. "Maybe ... dusky and risky."

He broke into full-on laughter. "Dusky and risky. Wow, I'll make sure to put that in my online dating profile."

I took a deep breath and slowly let it out.

"Uh oh, I see you're on your way down again."

"I'm sorry. I just feel like I should tell you that I'm not looking for anything right now. I tend to jump into things, and I know this sounds silly, but I'm on a journey to find myself. And I just can't do that if I'm

49

seeing someone. I tend to become whatever they want me to be. And right now, I need to find out exactly who I am."

He looked disappointed. "I understand. He reached into his wallet and pulled out a business card. "My cell number is on the back. Call me if you need anything while you're here . . . or when you get back to wherever you're from."

"Florida," I answered.

He smiled. "You may not know who you are, but I can tell. You're genuine. I don't come across very many people like that."

He picked up our bag of trash. "Maybe I'll run into you again before you head back to Florida."

I nodded and watched him walk away. Why did I feel so darn sad all of a sudden?

A shiny black car pulled up in the parking lot, and I could see through the rolled-down window that it was Grandma Dean. I made my way toward her, but hung back when I saw that she was still talking to Archer Nash. When she finally got out of the car, I walked over to her.

"How was lunch?" I asked.

She tried to keep a straight face, but she was failing miserably. Finally, she grinned. "It was lovely. Downright lovely."

I was about to ask where they had gone when a large pickup truck pulled into the parking lot, music blaring.

"Let me guess," Grandma said. "Hattie and Irene are just getting back from who-knows-where with who-knows-who."

But to our surprise, Greta and Virginia stepped out of the truck, giggling like schoolgirls. They waved at us, and we met them halfway.

"Where have you two been?" Grandma asked.

"Willie and Billie showed us the town," Virginia said, grinning from ear to ear. "We had a great time."

"What about you, Geraldine?" Greta asked. "How was your date?"

Grandma straightened up. "It wasn't a date. We got together to talk about Lou. And boy, do I have a lot to share with you ladies. Let's get Hattie and Irene and go sit somewhere quiet to talk."

"I don't think they're back yet," I said, looking around the parking lot.

"Oh, that's right," Virginia said, her face falling. "I gave them my keys. I guess we're stuck here until they get back."

Grandma looked at her phone. "It's nearly three o'clock. We promised that sweet girl we'd see her show again this evening and bring people with us. I'll text them and see where they are."

Grandma sent them a text, and surprisingly, they answered right away and said they'd head to the hotel.

Ten minutes later, we were still standing outside talking as they pulled in. I half expected them to be drunk and unruly, but to my surprise, they were . . . pleasant. Serene, almost.

Grandma Dean narrowed her eyes at them. "Are you on drugs?"

Hattie laughed. "Nothing more than we usually are."

There was something different about them, for sure, but we were all eager to hear what Grandma had learned about Lou. We climbed into the vehicle so Virginia could drive us around while Grandma told us what she had learned.

Before Grandma got started, Virginia held up a flyer. "You ladies want to check out the *Titanic* Museum? Geraldine can talk on the way there, and then maybe we can put some of Amy's flyers on some windshields or something."

We all agreed, and Virginia headed out of the parking lot.

"Okay, Geraldine," she said, looking at Grandma from the rearview mirror, "the floor is yours!"

Grandma Dean cleared her throat. "I think you all suspected what I'm about to say. I found out that Lou was murdered."

"Oh dear," Greta said, her hand over her heart. "I was afraid of that. What happened? Are there any suspects?"

"Archer Nash told me they think he was poisoned. He eats applesauce after every show, and he was eating it when he collapsed."

"Someone poisoned his applesauce?" I asked. "Who would do that?"

"They don't know yet," Grandma answered. "As careful as the murderer was, they did leave one thing behind—a long strand of blond-colored hair."

Greta looked concerned as she looked at Virginia. "Why didn't Billie or Willie tell us about that while we were with them today?"

"They might not have known yet," Grandma told them. "Archer said he called his friend at the sheriff's office this morning to see if there was any information yet, and they told him there wasn't any. But then they called him back right after he picked me up for lunch and told him the news. If Willie and Billie were out with you for a few hours, they might not have gotten the call. If they haven't heard yet, I'm sure they will soon."

"Poor guys," Virginia said. "One minute they seemed upbeat and the next they were grieving."

"It's really a testament to their faith," Greta added. "They believe he's in a better place, and I think that makes dealing with death a little easier."

"Yeah," Irene said dryly. "But it's one thing to go to that better place because it's your time. It's something entirely different if someone makes the decision for you."

"Did Archer know anyone that has long, blond hair?" Greta asked.

"He said he didn't," Grandma replied. "I saw a

picture of it. His friend at the police station sent it to him to see if he could identify it. It was just like he had described."

Whoever the killer was, they weren't at the table with us last night at the diner. No one there had blond-colored hair. But that made me think of a question. "Could the hair be from a wig?"

"It could be," Grandma answered. "They're going to analyze it and see if they can come up with any answers."

We were all quiet for a minute, and then Irene leaned toward the front seat. "So, Virginia, you're getting awfully cozy with Billie. Does that mean you're two timin' Hershel?"

I saw Virginia look up at Irene through the rear-view mirror. Even though I could only see the top half of her face, the wrinkles in her forehead and the sadness in her eyes told me things were not great between them.

"He dumped me," she said with a sigh.

We were all surprised.

"Oh Virginia," Greta said, putting her hand on Virginia's arm. "I'm so sorry. Do you want to talk about it?"

Virginia shrugged. "There's not much to talk about. He told me I was boring, and he needed something . . . someone . . . more exciting in his life."

"Does he know you're our getaway driver?" Hattie shrieked.

Virginia laughed. "No, I don't normally share that kind of information."

"Really?" Hattie asked, surprised. "I'd have that in my Tinder profile."

Irene chuckled. "Hattie, you also have your profession as a private eye."

"Really, Hattie?" Greta asked. "You know, just because you like to keep an eye on people's privates, that doesn't make you a private eye."

Hattie just shrugged. "Tomayto, tomahto."

Virginia pulled into the parking lot of the museum, and I was shocked at what I saw. Even though there was a picture of the museum on the brochure, it was still amazing to see in person. It looked like a giant ship.

Greta pulled a handful of Amy's flyers from her bag. "Okay," she said once we were out of the vehicle. "I don't know if this is legal or not, so we have to work fast." She divided the flyers between us, and we quickly put them on as many windshields as we could. Then we made our way into the museum.

Once we paid, we were given a boarding pass with the name and information of a real *Titanic* passenger. We were told at the end we could check one of the displays and see if our name was on the list of passengers who survived or the list of passengers who didn't. At first, it sounded like a fun game, but the more I walked through the museum and read about the passengers and what the ship

SHANNON VANBERGEN

was like, the heavier my heart became. Maybe it was because we were currently dealing with our own tragedy. Or maybe because it's a little morbid to walk around with a card that has a person's name on it, with the anticipation of finding out if they drowned or not. The grannies didn't seem to mind. They tucked their cards into their purses or pockets and enjoyed reading about the history of the *Titanic*.

An hour and a half later, we reached the room where we would find out our fate. I checked the name on my boarding pass and looked over the list of survivors on the wall.

"I survived!" I yelled out.

Greta cringed. "Well, I did too, but my whole family died."

I looked over at Grandma. "What about you?"

"I was onboard with my sister, and we both made it," Grandma answered.

"This is so depressing," Virginia said. "I made it, but I lost my husband."

I looked back at Hattie and Irene. "What about you guys?"

"We decided not to look," Hattie said. "We're just going to say that we married Leonardo DiCaprio and lived happily ever after."

"You know he dies in the movie, right?" I pointed out.

"Look," Irene said to me. "In our minds, this is a

56

Choose Your Own Adventure, and this is how we want it to play out."

Once outside, Grandma looked at her phone. "It's almost time for Amy's show. We can run by a drive-through and get some food, then head over to her makeshift theater."

So, that's what we did. When we pulled into the parking lot of the theater, there were a few other cars there already.

"Well, this is promising," Virginia said, pulling into a parking space.

We ate our food quickly, then made our way into the theater. By the time Amy started singing, there were fifteen of us in the audience.

Just like the day before, she sang her heart out, and she ended with a bow and a standing ovation.

"I really think she's got what it takes to make it here," Grandma said. "I just feel it in my bones."

"It's supposed to rain tomorrow," Irene said, nudging Grandma. "What you're feeling is arthritis."

Grandma Dean ignored her and walked up to Amy as she walked off the stage. "Somehow, you out did yourself from last night." Grandma told her.

"Thanks," Amy said, smiling. "It helps when there are more people in the audience."

"Well, we'll let you go talk to them," Grandma said, "but we'll try to be back to see your show tomorrow."

Amy thanked us, then walked over to greet her new fans.

"She's such a lovely girl," Virginia said as she walked away.

"You know," Greta said, "that other girl, Madison Paige, she's opening for some other act in town. If they still have tickets left, we can catch her."

We were all on board, so Greta pulled out her phone on the way to the SUV to see if she could get us tickets. "Done!" she exclaimed about the same time we finished buckling our seat belts. "Virginia, here's the address."

As Virginia drove to the next theater, Grandma's phone buzzed. "I just got a text from Archer Nash. He wants to know if we'd like to meet him and the gang at the diner again tonight."

"We don't have to drink root beer floats again, do we?" Irene asked. "As long as we don't, then I'm in."

"Me too," Virginia added.

Hattie surprised us all. "You know, I might have you drop me off at the hotel after the show."

Grandma's mouth fell open. "Are you feeling okay?"

"Yeah, now that I think about it, I think I'll pass too," Irene said, changing her mind. "Hattie and I are going out for breakfast early in the morning, so we shouldn't stay out too late."

"Okay," Greta said, turning from the front seat to look at them. "What are you two up to?"

"Nothing," they said at the same time.

"You two are never not up to something," Grandma added.

"Is it really that hard to believe that we want to get up early and enjoy a nice breakfast?" Irene asked.

"Yes!" we all said together.

Virginia looked at Irene from her rearview mirror. "I'm assuming you want to take my vehicle."

Hattie and Irene looked at each other. "Um, we don't know yet," Hattie answered. "We'll let you know."

Now we were really suspicious. Grandma gave me a look like she knew some kind of scheme was going on, and I gave her one right back.

We pulled up at the theater, and unlike the one Amy performed in, this was the real deal. Even with nearly thirty minutes to showtime, the parking lot was packed.

As we entered the building, my stomach suddenly felt like it was in knots. Last night at this time, we were walking into a theater expecting a great show, and we left seeing a dead body. I hoped this night wouldn't end the same.

7

THE SHOW WAS ABOUT to start, and the theater was full, though I'm guessing it had more to do with the main act, a family of seven who all played instruments and sang and danced. But I was curious to see just how talented the beautiful Madison Paige was.

The lights went down, and I felt excited for some reason. The stage was dazzling with a silver-and-blue metallic backdrop, but there wasn't a single instrument in sight. I never looked at the flyer, so I didn't even know what Madison did, other than sing Barbara Mandrell songs.

A light lit up center stage, and I heard the violin before I saw where the beautiful notes were coming from. Then Madison Paige came from the ceiling much the same way Archer Nash had done the night before. But instead of being on a platform, she was on a trapeze. Hanging upside down as she played, she swung in the air. I couldn't help but notice there was nothing on the stage to catch her if she fell. Another trapeze was pushed toward her from the side, and she was able to stop playing for just a moment, flip onto the other swinging bar, and continue playing.

I looked over to Grandma. "What is happening? What is this?"

Grandma whispered to me, "Apparently, she's an acrobat violinist. It didn't say anything about this in her flyer. It just showed her on stage singing."

She was lowered to the ground where she finished her song. The crowd cheered. She took a bow, and a large ribbon was lowered from the ceiling. She wrapped it around her waist and leg and then was hoisted into the air. While twirling, dropping, wrapping herself back up, going up in the air and back down again, she played and smiled her winning smile.

Eventually, she was standing on the stage again, and that's when she started singing. She sang mostly old country music. At some point, someone brought her a banjo which she played with high energy. Soon, the crowd was clapping along with her.

When it was over, Greta looked over at me and Grandma. "Wow! What a show! The instruments and the acrobats and the singing!"

Grandma shrugged. "Her violin playing was amazing. It reminded me a lot of Louise Mandrell, but if I had to choose a singer between her and Amy, I'd choose Amy."

"I agree," Virginia said, getting up. "Amy has the voice of an angel. But that Madison Paige," Virginia shook her head like she was still in disbelief, "she's an entertainer."

"Where are you going?" I asked as she scooted by us.

"I'm heading to the bathroom. There's no way this old bladder can hold on through another show."

The other grannies decided to go with her, so I sat by myself and kept watch over their sweaters and purses. I looked around and took in the architecture of the theater. It was a beautiful place—all wood with carvings along the walls. There was a balcony that looked like it was full of excited vacationers, all waiting to see the Seven Sven—the Swedish family that was the main show.

I felt my phone buzz in my pocket and saw that Owen was trying to call me. I sent him a quick text letting him know I couldn't talk because I was in a theater, but I would give him a call the next day. To my surprise, he texted back that he was hoping to talk tonight and wanted to know when I would get back to the hotel. I thought for a minute. The show wouldn't be over until ten o'clock, and we were meeting at the diner at eleven. I told him it would probably be after one in the morning before I got back. It took him two minutes to reply, but finally he said that was fine.

As I put my phone away, the grannies were coming back to their seats.

The lights were dimming as soon as they got

situated. I sat back in my seat, ready to see what the Seven Sven were all about. I just hoped it was entertaining enough to keep my mind off my future call with Owen. What could be so important that he would want to talk to me when I got back to the hotel well after midnight? I was afraid to find out.

8

"Isn't it amazing," Virginia said, driving toward our hotel, "how different the shows are here? The Seven Sven were nothing like I had ever seen before! What a talented family!"

"It was like *The Sound of Music* mixed with the Jackson Five . . . plus two more," Greta laughed.

"And Madison was amazing," I added. "I'm glad we ran into her after the show, and we got to talk to her for a minute."

Greta nodded. "I thought it was interesting that when we complimented her for making it big, she said she was still hoping to make it even bigger. Were you like that, Geraldine? Always wanting to make it bigger?"

"Oh yes," Grandma said with a sigh. "Success feels elusive even when you're living it. You reach your next goal, and before you even celebrate it, you're planning your next one."

We pulled into our parking lot, and Grandma leaned forward in her seat, putting her head between Hattie's and Irene's. "Are you sure you two don't want to come with us?"

Hattie fake yawned. "I need to hit the hay."

Irene unbuckled her seat belt. "Yeah, we need our beauty sleep. You gals have fun, though."

"Do you need my vehicle tomorrow . . . so you can go to breakfast?" Virginia looked at Hattie and Irene suspiciously.

They looked at each other. "No," Irene replied. "We'll call an Uber."

With that, they climbed out and walked up to the hotel. We watched as they disappeared inside their room.

"What do you think they're up to?" Grandma asked.

"I have no idea," Virginia said, driving us back out of the parking lot. "But I'm sure it's a doozy. It always is with those two."

Shortly before eleven, the guys came in the door of the diner, and soon the other performers from the night before filed in. I was surprised Roxy Rococo and the Kodiak King were there. I didn't expect them to show up. But one person was missing, Casius Nine.

"Thanks for letting me join you guys again tonight," Roxy said after ordering a sundae. "Have you heard anything about Lou?"

I looked over at Archer Nash. Would he tell her it was now a murder investigation? Instead, he glanced, and Billie and I caught the slightest shake of his head. Archer turned back to her. "No, we don't know anything yet."

Roxy slunk down in her chair. "When is the funeral? I'd be happy to sing something if you'd like."

Willie spoke up. "I think we're going to hold a memorial service next week at the theater. If you'd like to sing, we'd love that."

Then Kodiak King, whom everyone called Kodiak, leaned forward. "What was it like performing without him tonight?"

"Real hard," Billie answered. "I've got a good buddy that knows the routine in case one of us gets sick, and he steps in from time to time. Does a real good job. But it wasn't the same without Lou. We're going to have to hire someone else to permanently replace him. But I can't even think about that right now."

The table fell quiet for a moment, and I couldn't help but wonder where Casius was. I pulled out the card he had given me earlier and typed in his number. I sent him a text letting him know we were all at the diner if he wanted to join us. He responded immediately and said that he was on his way to Urgent Care. He had slipped in something wet behind the stage in between magic acts and hurt his ankle when he fell. He wanted to make sure it wasn't broken.

Since all the other grannies were paired off with a guy, I sat at the end next to Kodiak.

"Everything okay?" he asked me. "You look upset."

"I'm okay, but I just got a text from Casius. He's on his way to Urgent Care."

Billie heard me say his name. "Don't you believe anything that guy tells you. He lies more than a sack of dogs."

He went on ranting, but I didn't hear anything else he said. I was too busy picturing a sack of dogs.

Kodiak ignored Billie and turned to me again. "Is he all right?"

Billie was just ending his rant, and I didn't want him to start up again, so I just passed my phone to Kodiak so he could read it himself. He frowned and handed the phone back to me.

"You want to go check on him?" he asked me. "I can drive you over."

I shrugged. "I'm sure Casius has plenty of people there with him. I would just look silly showing up."

"Well, he's pretty much a loner, sticks to himself mostly. The only person he really counted on was Lou, and now that he's gone . . ." Kodiak went quiet.

"Maybe you should just drive over there, then," I said. "You know him. I would just feel weird if I went too."

He leaned close to me and nodded toward my

phone. "I've known him for years, and I don't have his number. If he gave it to you, then for some reason, he trusts you."

I sat there thinking about that for a minute. Why would he trust me? He didn't even know me. I looked up at Kodiak. "You're okay if I ride along?"

He clapped me on the back so hard I thought my teeth were going to fall out. "Let's ride!"

I walked over to Grandma and whispered to her what was going on, and she told me to give her an update as soon as I could. When I got to the door, I looked at them, all huddled around a table in the back. Greta sitting next to Willie, laughing about something. Virginia leaned in close to Billie as he told her some crazy story. And Grandma and Archer Nash sitting at the head of the table, each the leader of their own group. He put his arm around her and said something that made her laugh. My heart swelled. They had lived their lives, had their husbands, and now it was like they were starting all over again. They looked so happy. But as I turned to go out the door, something else caught my eye. Roxy Rococo giving Grandma a cold, hard stare. Suddenly, I didn't trust her, and I made a promise to keep my eye on her.

9

KODIAK OPENED the door of his truck for me. Climbing up into it was quite a job. Finally, I was in, and we were on our way across town.

"So," I said to end the awkward silence. "What happened to your eye?"

He looked confused and then he pointed to his eyepatch. "Oh, this?"

To my shock and horror, he ripped off the patch and looked at me. I tried to brace myself for what I was about to see. But then I was confused.

"You look totally fine!" I yelled, then hit him in the arm for scaring me. "Why do you even wear that thing?!"

He let out a deep and hearty laugh which made me laugh. "It's a crazy story."

"Well, now you have to tell me!" I insisted.

"Okay, well, when I first started out here, I was just

opening for other small acts, but I really wanted to have my own show. You have to start small and work your way up. So, my next plan was to open for a bigger show. But no one wanted a big, burly man who makes animals do tricks.

"Then one day, I was out driving in the country, heading to my little ranch, and I decided to open my truck window. As soon as I rolled it down, something struck me in the face. I drove off the road and came to a stop in a field."

"Oh my gosh! What was it?" I asked.

"I didn't know at the time. All I knew was that my face was bloody, and I was disoriented. It took me a minute to realize my nose was broken. I have some real nice neighbors, and one saw me crash through their fence, so he came to see if I was okay. He took one look at me and made me scoot over to where you're sitting, and he drove me to the hospital."

"That was so nice of him," I said, in shock over his story. "What was wrong with your eye?"

"Whatever flew through my window hit me in the eye and scratched my cornea. It also cut just below my eyebrow, and I had to have stitches. It broke my nose, and I had a concussion."

"Did you ever find out what hit you?"

He nodded. "It turned out the reason my neighbor saw me drive through his fence was because he was out there shooting doves. I just happened to drive by as he shot one, and when I rolled down the window of my truck, it got sucked in and hit me in the face. We found it in the back seat."

"No way," I said, laughing. "There is no way that's a true story."

"I'm telling you! That's what happened! I had the dang thing stuffed, and I keep it on my fireplace. It ended up being my good luck charm! After that, people took me more seriously. It turns out people think an animal trainer is more interesting if they think he lost an eye. So now I keep the patch on during my shows or when I'm out in public. I take it off otherwise."

"That is crazy!" I laughed.

After a minute or so, Kodiak grew serious. "I'm going to tell you something, and I don't want it to leave this truck."

That didn't sound good. "Okay," I promised.

He stared out the windshield. "I heard that Lou was murdered."

I pretended to be surprised, but he shifted his eyes to me without moving his head. "You heard already?"

"Am I that obvious?"

He gave me a look that said yes, I was that obvious.

"So, who do you think did it?" I asked.

He grew uneasy. "I don't know if I should say."

"Oh, come on," I begged. "You can tell me."

"All right, but this is just a feeling. I don't have any evidence or anything."

I nervously bit my lip, waiting for him to tell me. But I was definitely not prepared for his answer.

He looked at me, his eyes filled with sadness. "I think it might have been Archer Nash."

"What!?" I practically yelled. "Why would you think that?"

"Now, just calm down. I know your mee-maw is into him and everything . . ."

"My mee-maw?" Grandma Dean would have a fit if she heard him call her that. "First of all, that is not what we call her. She is my mother's mother!" What in the world was wrong with me? As soon as those words left my mouth, I felt like a crazy woman had taken over my brain and was overriding any kind of rational thought. "And secondly, she's not into him. She used to be an entertainer herself, and she is just enjoying the company of a fellow performer!"

He threw his hands up in the air. "I wasn't tryin' to be disrespectful. I have a mee-maw. Geesh, it's an endearing name. You act like I called her the worst thing in the world. My mee-maw would fight tooth and nail to keep that title!"

I took a deep breath. Why was I getting so upset?

"I'm sorry," I said to him after collecting myself. "You can tell me why you think Archer Nash would murder Lou."

"Forget it," he said looking over at me, still in shock over my outburst. "I don't want to talk about it if you're going to bite my head off."

"I said I was sorry! I don't even know why that upset me. I guess I'm just overly protective of my grandma. And if you think he's really a murderer and then I just left her with him . . . well, it just freaked me out, I guess."

We sat there quietly for a minute, and I could tell he was debating on telling me. Finally, he let out a big breath. "I'm afraid that if you get upset that easily, you're really going to be upset with me after I tell you the next thing."

"Just tell me," I urged. "I'll handle it better. I promise."

"Well," he said slowly. "Here's the deal. I know that Archer Nash and Roxy Rococo used to have some kind of thing going on between them."

"Thing?" I asked. "What kind of thing?"

He seemed nervous. "You know, a personal thing."

"They were dating?"

"Yeah, I don't know how serious they were, but I know it went on for a while. Like a couple of years."

Years? Well, that sounded pretty serious to me.

"Lou always liked Roxy. He was always hitting on her and asking her out. She and Archer tried to keep things between them a secret, but we all knew, so Lou had to know too. But he had eyes for her anyway. Then last week, I saw something I shouldn't have."

"What?" I asked as my stomach did a little nervous flip-flop.

He paused and let out another deep breath. "We were all at the diner after the show. Lou got up to go to the bathroom, and a few minutes later, Roxy got up too. I didn't think nothin' about it. But then I decided to go too."

He stopped and looked at me. "It's not weird or anything. It's a multiple person bathroom."

I rolled my eyes. "I didn't think it was weird. Go on."

"Well, I turned to go down the hall toward the bathrooms, and I saw them making out in the hallway. I felt all embarrassed seeing them like that. I turned around to go back to the table, and I ran right into Archer. He saw the whole thing."

"Wait," I said, leaning forward. "Are Archer and Roxy still dating?"

He shrugged. "I don't know. But I never heard for sure that they broke up."

I tried to take in this information, make sense of it all. "Did Archer seem upset when you were all back at the table?"

Kodiak shrugged again. "He was quiet, that was for sure."

"So, you think he might have killed Lou in some fit of jealousy?"

"I'm not saying nothin' for sure," he said. "I'm just sayin' it's a possibility."

I felt sick to my stomach. I was going to have to tell Grandma Dean. I sent her a quick text. "Don't do anything alone with Archer Nash. We need to talk later."

I put my phone down just as we were pulling into

the parking lot at Urgent Care. I recognized Casius' car by the front door. I wanted to help my new friend, but I also wanted to be by Grandma's side to protect her from a possible killer.

My phone buzzed, and it was Grandma Dean. Her reply made my blood go cold.

"Wish you would've sent that five minutes earlier..."

10

I SENT Grandma another text and asked her where she was. I got nervous when she didn't answer right away, so I sent a text to Virginia and Greta asking if they knew where she was. I hoped that someone would text me back soon.

Kodiak put his eyepatch back on, and we headed to the doors of Urgent Care. When we walked in, I could see Casius sitting in the waiting room. He was surprised to see us.

"What are you two doing here?" He tried to act like he wasn't happy to see us, but I could tell he was.

I walked over to him. "Let's see your ankle. How bad is it?"

He was still wearing his clothes from the show— black suit with a purple shirt. He was even wearing a cape. The outfit was nice, but the cape made me chuckle inside. He lifted up a pant leg, and Kodiak and I gasped.

"Dude, that's friggin' broke," Kodiak said. "Even with one eye, I can see that."

Casius looked up at him. "One eye, huh?"

"How exactly did this happen?" I asked.

Casius dropped his pant leg and sat back up in his chair. "I did a disappearing act, and I hid off stage for a minute. When it was time to go back on, I slipped on something wet by the stairs that led back up to the stage. I twisted my ankle when I fell. It's so dark back there, I didn't even see it."

That sounded suspicious to me. "What was it? What did you slip on?"

"I think it was dog pee. I had a dog with me, and I think when we were waiting backstage, it might have relieved itself."

"Why do you have a dog in your show?" I asked.

"People go crazy over animals. I can do a disappearing act, and people will clap. I can do the same thing with a dog, and people will give me a standing ovation." He smiled. "Plus, I like dogs."

Kodiak laughed. "You come across like you're so scary, but really you're just a softy."

I sat down on the other side of him. "Did you finish the show like this?"

"Well, yeah. Those people paid a lot of money to see the show tonight. Plus, if I didn't go back on, it would ruin the illusion. I wasn't about to do that."

A nurse brought out a wheelchair and pulled it up in front of Casius. "Are you ready Mr. Nine?"

That sounded so strange. I'd have to ask him if that was really his last name. I was becoming intrigued by stage names. It was almost like these people led double lives.

Once Casius was in the wheelchair, I patted his leg. "Good luck. I'm sure you're in good hands."

The nurse smiled. "The best! We'll have you all fixed up before you can say 'Abracadabra'!"

Casius rolled his eyes, and thankfully, the nurse was already standing behind him, so she didn't see. I couldn't help but chuckle. The life of a magician seemed anything but magical.

We watched Casius as he was wheeled through the waiting room and disappeared behind a set of double doors.

I looked over at Kodiak. "Is his last name really Nine?"

He laughed so hard, he snorted. "No. It's Usldinger."

I cringed. "Yikes. No wonder he changed it. I wonder how he came up with the last name Nine."

"His real last name has nine letters," Kodiak answered. "For a magician, he's not very creative."

I thought Casius Nine had a nice ring to it.

"So, what's your real name?" I asked. "Surely, it's not really Kodiak."

He moved over into Casius' old seat and dropped

his voice so no one else would here. "Brent Davis. But don't tell anyone."

"Brent," I repeated in a whisper.

"Yeah, but Kodiak has been my nickname for years. I was obsessed with bears when I was a kid."

"Do you have them in your show?"

"Nah, too dangerous. But I do have an alligator. And I have wildlife that's a little tamer—snakes, lizards, a couple of racoons . . . small things I can bring on a stage."

I furrowed my brows. "Aren't people upset there's not a bear?"

Now he looked upset. "I never promised anyone a bear. But I'll show you what I do have. Look at this."

He pulled out his phone and handed it to me. I watched a video of a dog jumping rope, a cat jumping through swinging hoola hoops, and a pony playing a song on a piano.

"You're smiling," he said, "so that must mean you like it?"

"Is this part of your show?"

"Yeah. I've always loved animals," he answered. "And it's so fun to work with them every day. I like to get them from rescue places and give them a good home and train them. Sometimes, I look at these animals that people have discarded, and I'm blown away by their intelligence. Animals are smarter than people, if you ask me."

"Where do you keep all of these animals?" I asked.

He smiled. "At my ranch just outside of town. I have a whole zoo out there." Kodiak nodded toward the door that Casius had walked through. "Casius gets his animals from me. He's real good with them."

My phone buzzed, and it was a text from Grandma saying she was back at the hotel. Archer had just dropped her off.

"Want me to take you back to your hotel?" he asked. "It's awfully late."

I sat there, torn.

"I'll tell you what, I'll take you to your hotel and come back here and wait for Casius. One of us will text you and let you know what happened with his ankle, though I can guarantee you, the news won't be good."

I still felt bad leaving, but I wanted to talk to Grandma before she went to sleep. Plus, I still needed to call Owen. I walked out the door, hoping for the best for all of us.

———

"How's Casius?" Grandma asked as soon as I walked into our hotel room.

I shrugged. "He's getting an x-ray, but Kodiak is pretty sure his ankle is broken. What happened with you and Archer tonight? Where did you two go off to?"

Grandma was sitting in bed working on a word search, and she put her pencil down and closed the book. "He just took me home. Willie and Billie invited Greta and Virginia to some lookout."

I cringed. "To a lookout or to make out?"

Grandma chuckled. "I don't even want to think about it. It's like those two have turned into Hattie and Irene."

I sighed and sat down in a chair in the corner. The lamp by Grandma's bed was emitting a soft, golden light in the otherwise dark room. The air conditioning unit was quietly humming along next to me. and my eyelids started to droop. I was exhausted. But there was something I needed to tell Grandma Dean.

"So, I guess I should tell you what I learned about Archer Nash tonight," I started.

"That he was dating Roxy Rococo?" Grandma asked.

I sat up straight, the exhaustion leaving my body. "You knew about that?"

Grandma nodded. "I couldn't help but notice the dirty looks she was giving me, so I asked Archer about it on the ride home."

I sat back in my chair. False alarm, the exhaustion was still there.

"Are they still together or did they break up?" I asked.

Grandma leaned over and put her word search book on her nightstand. "He says they broke up months ago."

"Do you believe him?"

"It doesn't really matter, does it? I'm just here to . . ."

She stopped mid-sentence and stared at her lap.

I walked over and sat on the edge of her bed. "You know it's okay if you start dating again. As long as he's not a killer, he'd make a great boyfriend."

"Who knows," Grandma said, sliding under the covers, "maybe he is."

"A great boyfriend?" I asked.

"No," Grandma said, closing her eyes. "A killer."

11

I COULD TELL Grandma didn't want to talk anymore, so I reached over and turned off her light. I grabbed my phone and went into the bathroom so I didn't disturb her while I called Owen.

I made myself comfy in the bathtub and looked at my phone. It was one thirty in the morning. That seemed too late to call Owen. Maybe I would just text him instead. I sent a quick text and asked if he was still awake. While I waited for his answer, I looked up at the ceiling. I wondered what Grandma really thought about Archer. They seemed to have an instant connection. The way they talked and laughed. They had only known each other for a short time, but they already seemed to be comfortable and at ease with one another. Maybe it was something in the Branson air. Virginia and Greta certainly felt comfortable with Willie and Billie. And in some way, I even felt comfortable around Casius and Kodiak. Maybe that's just how people felt when they weren't being smothered with humidity. But then I thought about Roxy. I definitely didn't feel comfortable around her.

My phone rang, and I answered it as quickly as I could so it wouldn't wake Grandma.

"I can't believe you're still up," I said to Owen.

He sounded exhausted. "I can't either. But I wanted to talk to you. We didn't get a chance to talk before you left."

I wanted to say that I had been available to talk before we left, but he didn't seem to be. But I kept my mouth shut. We were both tired, and I knew that would just start some sort of argument that neither of us had the energy for.

"How's Branson?" he asked.

I should've just said, "Fine," and then let him do all the talking so I would know why he wanted to chat so late at night. But no. Maybe it was the exhaustion, maybe it was the trauma of seeing Lou, or maybe it was the emotional stress I had over Grandma coming face to face with Thomas (if she ever got up the nerve to go to his house), but whatever it was, I burst into tears. "Lou is dead, Casius possibly broke his ankle because he slipped in pee between magic acts, and did you know that if a bird is falling from the sky and you open your car window at that moment, it could get sucked in and hit you in the face?!"

Owen was silent for a minute. "Have you been

drinking? Did someone give you moonshine? I heard that's popular up there."

"No," I sniffed. "I haven't been drinking."

"Is it drugs, then?" he asked. "Because at this point, I'm hoping it's drugs."

"It's not drugs," I said wiping my face.

"Who is Lou, who is Casius, and why are you worried about birds falling from the sky?"

I filled him in on everything that had happened in the short amount of time we had been there—Lou's death, Greta and Virginia acting like Hattie and Irene, and Hattie and Irene being up to something, but we didn't know what that was yet.

He listened quietly while I explained everything. Finally, he spoke. "So, this Lou guy . . . you guys are leaving the investigation up to the police, right?"

"Of course," I said, like that was a crazy question to even ask. "We are staying out of it. I might have questioned Casius a little bit, and I might have a few things I want to talk to Kodiak about. And of course, Grandma is getting some information here and there from Archer. But other than that, we're staying out of it." I sighed. "Besides, I kind of feel like I'm on my own here. I'm the only one who hasn't paired off with someone."

"Is that a bad thing?" Owen asked quietly. "If anything, that shows real growth on your part . . . right?"

I couldn't help but laugh. "Is this what growth feels like? Because it's pretty awful."

Owen laughed too, but then he became serious. "I know you and I are in this weird place right now, and we haven't really had a chance to talk about us or where we're headed, but I hope we can do that when you get back. I miss you."

I was quiet. For the first time in as long as I could remember, I felt content being single.

I didn't want to hurt Owen's feelings, so I told him we'd talk when I got back. If he noticed any apprehension in my voice, he didn't let on.

We ended our call, and I closed my eyes. I was fully dressed, lying in a bathtub in Branson, Missouri wondering who killed Lou and how Casius was doing at the Urgent Care. Then my phone buzzed. It was a text from Kodiak. "Yep, I called it. It's broken."

At least that answered one question.

THE NEXT MORNING, Grandma Dean burst in the door followed by Greta and Virginia. My heart was pounding as I looked at the clock. Eleven thirty in the morning.

"You guys nearly scared me to death!" I said, sitting up in bed. "What a terrible way to wake up! What's going on?"

Grandma was pacing, which was very unlike her. "I don't even know what to tell you first."

I looked at Virginia and Greta, hoping they would fill me in, but they looked just as concerned as Grandma.

"Will somebody please tell me something?!"

Grandma looked at me, her arms crossed. "First of all, I had breakfast with Archer this morning, but I stopped by Hattie and Irene's room first. I knocked and knocked, and there was no answer."

"Well, they said they were going to go to breakfast this morning," I reminded Grandma.

"Did they go to breakfast?" Virginia asked. "Or did they leave sometime last night, and they're not back yet?"

"We're afraid they're missing," Greta answered. "We've texted them several times, and they haven't answered. We're worried sick about them."

"I'm sure they're fine," I tried to reassure them . . . and maybe myself. "Maybe Paulette saw them this morning. You know how much Hattie loves the koi pond. Did you check with her?"

The grannies all looked at one another. Judging by their faces, they hadn't.

"Let's go," Grandma said. She opened a dresser drawer and pulled out some clothes for me. "Get dressed. We're going to go look for them. We'll start with Paulette."

I got dressed and quickly brushed my hair. Grandma must have really been concerned about Hattie and Irene because she didn't even lecture me on my lack of makeup.

We opened the door of the hotel and were greeted by the ever-smiling Paulette. "Well, hello ladies!" she said. "What can I do for you?"

Grandma walked over to the counter. "Did you see two of our friends this morning? Did they by chance come in here?"

Paulette looked us over like she was trying to figure

out who was missing. Then she smiled. "Oh yes, the two that talk like sailors?"

"Yes," Grandma said, relieved. "They were here this morning?"

Paulette nodded. "They came in and asked if I had any coffee filters. They said they needed two. I gave them a couple, and they took them to the bathroom with them. When they came out, they saw a truck outside, and they seemed excited and ran out."

Grandma turned to us and sighed. "Who knows what men those two have gotten involved with?"

"Oh no," Paulette said shaking her head. "I saw two women in the truck, not men."

We looked at each other, confused. Women? And what was up with the coffee filters?

Just then, Greta's phone buzzed. "It's Hattie!" she squealed. "She just sent me a text."

"You tell her she needs to come back to the hotel right away," Grandma scolded. "I got some information today that we all need to discuss."

Greta's thumbs went crazy typing. The woman texted like a teenager. Then she looked up and smiled. "They're on their way."

We were waiting in Virginia's SUV when they got there. We saw a truck pull up, and the two of them got out. As they walked over to us, I noticed both of them folding something white and putting it in their purses. It was round . . . could it be a coffee filter?

They were all smiles when they got in and hooked their seat belts.

Greta turned around from the front seat and narrowed her eyes at them. "Would you two ladies like to tell us where you've been?"

Hattie and Irene looked at each other, then back at Greta. "We had breakfast," Irene said. "That's not illegal here in Branson, is it?"

"You had breakfast?" Greta asked. "Why didn't you answer your phone when we texted you?"

Hattie gave us an innocent look. "Irene left her phone in our room, and I have my ring tone set to birds chirping. Do you know how hard it is to tell the difference between real birds and a bird ring tone?"

"Then why don't you change it?" Virginia asked.

"Why would I do that?" Hattie asked.

I didn't know if Hattie truly didn't see the problem with it or if she was trying to avoid answering the question, but either way, we moved on.

"So, what's the problem?" Irene asked. "Why did we have to come rushing back?"

"I'll tell you over lunch," Grandma said. "Virginia, let's ride."

We all decided we wanted to go back to that pizza place again, and in ten minutes, we were pulling up in the parking lot. After piling our plates high with pizza and a little salad, we sat back down in the booth we had been in the first day we arrived.

90

Greta placed a napkin on her lap. "So, Geraldine, what's going on?"

Grandma took a sip of her tea then looked around to make sure no one was listening. "Lou was poisoned, for sure. You know how Willie and Billie said Lou always ate applesauce after the show? Well, someone added some antifreeze."

"Antifreeze won't kill you!" Hattie exclaimed. "I used to put a little in my husband's coffee when we ran out of sugar."

Our mouths dropped open in horror. "Hattie," I said, "antifreeze will too kill you!"

She shrugged and smiled. I made a mental note to find out why Hattie's husband was no longer around.

"It wasn't just that one container," Grandma continued. "They tested all the containers of applesauce in the mini-fridge in his dressing room, and they all contained antifreeze."

"Did someone make him the applesauce or was it store-bought?" Virginia asked.

"Store-bought," Grandma answered. "But the silver foil on each container was pulled back a bit in one corner. It was obviously tampered with."

"Who would do that?" I asked. "All the entertainers have alibis, right? Kodiak, Casius, Roxy, they all had shows that night."

"And Archer was on stage," Greta added.

"Willie and Billie said they watched Archer's show

that night," Virginia said. "Do we know if their alibis check out?"

Grandma nodded. "Yes, Archer said the police were able to confirm it. But here's the thing. We don't know when the applesauce was tampered with and put in his mini fridge. The antifreeze could've been there for days. The murderer didn't even have to be there that night."

That meant that their alibis didn't mean anything, but it also meant that the murderer could be anybody. "Someone at a grocery store could've done it," I suggested.

"That's terrible," Greta said shaking her head. "Poor Lou."

"Did they analyze the blond hair they found on him?" Irene asked.

"Yes," Grandma said pulling out her phone. "And they found several more. It turns out, it's not human hair."

"It's not?" Irene asked. "What is it?"

"Horsehair," Grandma said, handing Irene her phone. "This is the picture Archer was able to get from his detective friend."

Irene looked at the picture, and Hattie leaned over and looked at it too. Then it was passed to Virginia, then Greta.

"Does Lou have horses?" Greta asked, holding the phone.

"He's afraid of them," I answered, remembering the

story Billie had told us the night he died.

Greta passed the phone to me, and my heart sank a little. That color looked very familiar. "Grandma, does it have to be a horse's hair? Could it be from a pony?"

"I suppose so," she said. "Why is that?"

"Because," I answered, my heart heavy. "Kodiak showed me a video of his piano-playing pony last night, and this was the color of its hair."

Grandma took her phone and looked around the table. "Look at us," she said. "A man is dead, and while the rest of us are running off with men like a bunch of teenyboppers, Nikki is the only one actually gathering evidence. Did you ladies know that she has questioned both Casius and Kodiak?"

The grannies looked guilty.

"I'm sorry," Greta said. "I got caught up in all the attention I was getting."

"Me too," Virginia said.

We looked at Hattie and Irene.

"Don't look at us," Irene said. "We've been angels."

Irene winked. "Though I would like to see that video of Kodiak's pony playing the piano."

"It's an actual pony," I told her, rolling my eyes.

Hattie and Irene snickered like middle schoolers.

"We're all sorry," Grandma said. "The only way we're going to solve this is if we work together."

"I don't mean to interrupt," Greta said. "But isn't that Amy over there?" We followed Greta's gaze, and sure enough, she was back again, handing out more flyers.

"That poor girl," Grandma said. "She's trying so hard to get herself an audience."

Grandma waved her over when she looked our way. For some reason, she looked nervous when she saw us. Something she had said the first time we met her stood out in my mind. I could hear her voice echo in my head. "I would do anything to make it out here." Could that mean murder?

AMY JOINED us at the table, and Grandma invited her to sit with us.

She put her head in her hands. "I'm exhausted. I spend all day handing out flyers, then I perform, then I have to deal with the stress of my bandmates, and some people in this town are just crazy and are trying to make my already miserable life even more miserable." She looked up at all of us. "I'm sorry. I don't even really know you amazing ladies, and now I'm unloading all my problems onto you."

Greta patted her on the back. "That's okay. We're here for you."

"And we're coming to your show tonight, aren't we, girls!" Greta said with enthusiasm.

Irene glanced at Hattie. "Well, actually, Hattie and I have plans. But the rest of you go on."

"Great!" Amy said, dropping her face back into her

hands and rubbing her temples. "There goes half of my audience." She looked up at us with tears in her eyes. "The guys are going to quit on me. They can't handle this anymore. This is so much harder than we ever thought it would be."

"You can't give up!" Greta encouraged. "We'll help you get the word out."

Amy sighed. "Maybe I need to change things up a little bit. I mostly just sing. I can play the piano and the banjo. Maybe I need to incorporate that into my show . . . while I jump through a fire on a unicycle or something."

"You don't need to rely on gimmicks," Grandma told her. "But if you could play those other instruments during your show, I bet it would draw in more people."

I couldn't let the whole banjo thing go. That was what Lou played. Could she have killed him in hopes of taking his spot?

"So," I asked. "How well do you play the banjo?"

Amy shrugged. "Pretty well. It's probably my favorite instrument to play."

Virginia perked up. "Then you should have that in your show! It's so fun to watch someone play the banjo." Her face fell. "I know we enjoyed watching Lou play the other night."

I watched Amy's reaction as Virginia mentioned Lou. For just a moment, her eyes got bigger, and that nervousness returned. Something was there—was it guilt?

"Do you have horses?" I asked her.

All eyes were suddenly on me, and the grannies looked shocked. They knew what I was up to, and they didn't like it.

"Ha!" Amy scoffed. "I can barely feed myself. There's no way I could afford a horse."

Now Grandma really looked concerned. "How are you making ends meet?"

Amy sighed and rubbed her temples. "I work nights at a twenty-four-seven grocery store across town. I make minimum wage, but it at least pays the rent."

Now the grannies looked concerned too.

"Did you know Lou?" I asked. "Had you ever met him before?"

Exhausted Amy quickly turned to anxious Amy. She stood up and stuttered like her mouth and brain were in an argument about what to say next, and neither of them were winning.

"I met him once," she finally managed to say. "I better get going. I have some more flyers to hand out before the show. Maybe I'll see you tonight?"

We nodded and told her goodbye. Instead of handing out more flyers in the restaurant, Amy walked out.

"Well, that was strange. Don't you think?" I asked the grannies.

"I hate to admit it," Grandma said slowly. "But something with her didn't seem right."

"She got awfully nervous when she was asked about Lou," Greta pointed out.

"But she doesn't own a horse," Irene added.

Then all eyes were on her and Hattie.

"And why can't you two join us for Amy's performance tonight?" asked Grandma. "Where are you two running off to?"

"We have plans," Hattie said with a smile. "Don't wait up!"

Grandma rolled her eyes. Whatever those two crazy women were up to, they weren't going to let us in on it.

Grandma brought the conversation back to the case. "Nikki, is Kodiak going to the diner tonight after his show?"

"I don't know," I answered. "I haven't heard from him all day."

"If he is, maybe you can figure out where he lives. Maybe you can make plans to go to his place . . ."

"Oh no," I said shaking my head. "My seducing days are over. Plus, he seems like a really nice guy, and I don't want to lead him on."

"Well, how else are we going to get close to him?" Greta asked. "I can ask Willie where Kodiak lives, but we need to be able to get on his property."

Irene leaned forward. "I think we should look into Amy. She works at a grocery store, so she could've done something to the applesauce."

"But what's her motive?" Greta asked.

"Maybe she wanted to steal his spot in the group,"

Irene suggested. "Or maybe she was targeting someone else, and Lou just happened to buy the wrong container of applesauce. She did have the ability to tamper with it. And she acted strange when Lou's name was brought up."

I didn't want to bring it up, but Archer Nash was a suspect on my list. I decided to keep it to myself, but Grandma surprised me by bringing it up.

"If we're making a suspect list, I think we should add Archer Nash," Grandma said, looking disappointed. "Nikki and I found out that he and Roxy had been dating, and apparently she had a fling with Lou a couple of weeks ago."

The other grannies were shocked. "Oh Geraldine," Greta said. "I'm so sorry."

She huffed. "It's not like we're dating, Greta. I just met the guy. We're just developing a friendship. That's all."

By now, Virginia had taken a notebook and pen out of her purse and was jotting all of this down. "So, Archer had access to the applesauce, and he had a motive. What about Kodiak? What is his motive? He has his own successful show. All we have on him so far is he had a pony with the same color hair found at the crime scene. That hardly makes him a killer."

"I don't know," I said. "But maybe we should add Casius. Billie can't stand him and thinks he's the murderer." Then I thought of something. "Last night at Urgent Care, Kodiak mentioned that sometimes Casius borrows animals from him to use in his shows. What if he borrowed the pony?"

Grandma sighed. "And make sure you add Amy."

"I would love to compare our list of suspects to the local police's list," Irene said.

Grandma looked at us. "I've seen the list."

That surprised all of us. I knew Grandma was getting all kinds of information from Archer that he was getting from his friend at the station, but this was the first I had heard of possible suspects.

"Who's on the list?" I asked.

"Just one person," Grandma answered. "And you're not going to be happy when you hear who it is."

"WHO IS IT?" I asked again.

Grandma looked at Virginia. "I'm sorry, Virginia, but it's Billie."

"Billie?" We all yelled out, getting looks from the people seated around us.

"Don't ask me why," Grandma said. "Because I don't know. All I know is there was a family dispute."

Virginia's pen hovered over the paper, unable to write down his name.

Irene slid the paper from Virginia and gently took the pen. She wrote down his name, then looked up at us. "We've got a long list here. Let's start knocking off some names. Let's start with Kodiak. We need to get on his property and check out that pony. Hattie and I can help you do that."

Hattie crossed her arms and huffed. "We've got a good thing going, Irene. You're going to mess it all up."

"We'll be fine," Irene answered. "Once we do that, Nikki can question Casius again. You can check on him and see how his ankle is doing. That gives you a way in. Find out if he ever used the pony in one of his shows and how recently that was. Also, find out what really happened between him and Lou."

"Got it," I answered. Normally, it was Grandma who took charge and gave orders. It was interesting to see Irene take over.

"Geraldine, you question Archer Nash. Find out what you can about him and Roxy. See if you can figure out how serious they were."

Grandma nodded.

"Greta, Virginia, you two need to find out what kind of family dispute the police are talking about, but you need to do it without tipping your hand."

Virginia stayed silent, but Greta answered for the both of them. "We're on it."

"That leaves Amy," Irene said. "Can you gals talk to her tonight? See if you can figure out her connection to Lou."

"This all sounds great," Grandma said, sitting forward and crossing her hands on the table. "But how are you going to get us on Kodiak's property?"

Hattie looked at Irene like she was silently pleading with her not to tell.

"I'm sorry, Hattie," Irene said. "You know it's the right thing."

"Fine," Hattie murmured.

Irene nervously cleared her throat. "Hattie and I have become . . . friends . . . with the people who live next door to Kodiak."

"I don't want details," Grandma said, shaking her head.

"It's not what you think," Hattie said.

"No," Grandma answered. "It's probably worse than I think."

Irene wrote something on the bottom of the suspect list and tore off the corner. "Here," she said handing the paper to Grandma. "Meet us at this address tonight after Amy's performance, but before you go to the diner. We'll get you on the property, you can check out the pony, and be back in time for a round of root beer floats at the diner when the guys get there."

Half an hour later, we were dropping off Hattie and Irene in the hotel parking lot.

"It's only two o'clock," Virginia said. "We could go do some sightseeing. Or we could go see Thomas, and . . ."

"I'm not ready to see Thomas," Grandma interrupted. "Besides, Hattie and Irene would be very upset if we went without them."

Even though I felt like Grandma Dean was just stalling, I knew she was right about Hattie and Irene.

"Well," Greta answered. "We could visit the wax museum. That looks fun!"

We all agreed, and soon, we were pulling into the parking lot, marveling over the cool building. Once inside, we got our picture taken and, thanks to a green screen, it looked like King Kong was holding us in his hands while he climbed a building. As we started to walk through the exhibit, I marveled over the picture. We were all acting like we were screaming, and I couldn't help but laugh at it. The grannies were so young at heart. They were over twice my age, but they sure didn't act like it.

We meandered through the wax museum, stopping to take pictures of each other with Michael Jackson, Hugh Hefner, and the guys from Star Trek. Then we decided to head over to the Ripley's Believe It or Not! Museum where we walked around for another hour. By the time we were done, the grannies wanted to head back to the hotel and shower before Amy's show. Even though they didn't seem tired, I was exhausted. And before I traipsed all over Kodiak's property in the dark, I needed a nap. But could I calm my nerves enough to actually sleep?

15

I SNUGGLED under the covers while I listened to water running in the bathroom. Grandma was showering, and I had pulled the bedroom curtains closed to make the room as dark as possible. But still I couldn't sleep. I couldn't stop my mind from wandering—first to Casius and his ankle, then to Kodiak and his property, and finally to Owen and his silence after our phone call the other night. As if he knew I was thinking about him, Owen sent me a text.

"Are you staying out of trouble?"

I was thankful he sent that text now and not in a few hours. I could honestly text back yes.

Grandma was soon out of the shower and dressed, and it was my turn in the bathroom. After a quick shower of my own, some gel in my hair, and a little makeup, I was ready to join the other grannies in the parking lot.

They all looked at me, concerned.

"You're not going to wear that to Kodiak's place, are you?" Grandma asked me.

I looked down at my coral sleeveless shirt. She was right. I wouldn't want to get it dirty. I looked at their own attire and was surprised that they were all in black. It looked like they were headed to a funeral instead of a show. I told them I'd be right back, and I ran back into my room. What could I wear that I wouldn't mind getting dirty? I had brought mostly nice clothes since I hadn't expected to scope out a farm when I packed for the trip. But then I remembered my yellow T-shirt from the zip line place. Perfect! I stuffed it into my purse and rejoined the grannies.

We sat through another one of Amy's beautiful performances, and I was anxious when it was over. We needed to get out of there quickly and drive out to meet Hattie and Irene, but first we had to figure out how Amy knew Lou. Grandma, Virginia, and I went to talk to her, while Greta walked over to talk to the band as they packed up for the night.

Grandma praised Amy for another job well done and then didn't waste any time asking her about Lou. Amy looked nervous and tried to avoid Grandma's questions. I heard laughter and looked over at Greta. She was pulling candy bars out of her purse and handing them to the guys. Greta was definitely a giver.

When we were back in the SUV, Virginia sighed. "Well, that was pointless. She seemed to avoid answering all of our questions about Lou. We didn't even figure out if she knew him."

"Oh, she knew him," Greta answered. "And if Lou had his way, she would've known him even better."

We all snapped to attention. "What do you mean?" I asked. "How do you know?"

Greta smiled. "The drummer sang like a bird. It's amazing what a little chocolate can do."

"What did he tell you?" Grandma asked.

"He said Amy and the band had a meeting with Lou about a week before he was murdered. Lou had agreed to listen to them and give them some advice or something. He said the whole time, Lou kept staring at Amy, and afterward, he asked her to stick around . . . alone."

"And she actually stayed?" I asked.

"The drummer said he let them sing on Archer's stage," Greta continued, "and Amy was enamored as soon as she got up there. They tried to talk her out of staying, but she said there wasn't any harm in her seeing what he had to say."

"What a slimeball," Virginia said, shaking her head.

"Yep," Greta answered. "Amy stayed but told the band later that Lou said he could help her career if she helped him first . . . if you get my drift."

"No wonder she acted strange when we brought up his name." Grandma shook her head. "Poor girl."

"Do you think that's enough of a motive?" I asked. "Or do you think one of her bandmates could've killed him? Maybe to get back at him or something?"

Grandma looked thoughtful. "I don't think so. She's trying to rise to the top. Why kill someone who claimed he could get you there? Even if he was a creep, she was able to walk out of there without him getting his hands on her. And as far as a band member, I don't know. It just doesn't feel right."

"None of this feels right," Virginia said as she left the parking lot.

I had to agree. We were missing so many pieces of this puzzle. I felt like we could possibly mark Amy off our long suspect list. But I wasn't completely ready to do that yet.

It took twenty minutes to drive to the address Irene had given us, and when we pulled up in front of a big farmhouse, Hattie and Irene were waiting on the front porch.

We got out of the vehicle, and Grandma looked over at me. "Don't forget, you need to change."

"Oh, that's right," I said, pulling the bright yellow shirt from my purse.

"What is that?" Grandma asked.

I looked up to see all eyes on me, and they didn't look happy.

I held up the shirt. "What's wrong with it? It's the only shirt I didn't mind if it got a little dirty."

"We don't care if it gets dirty!" Irene said with a hiss. "We're going undercover in the night! You need to wear something dark! You put that on, and you'll stand out like a beacon!"

Oh. This whole snooping around thing was still a bit new to me.

"Here," Hattie said, fishing around in her purse. "Wear this."

She pulled out a one-piece leopard-print bodysuit.

"No way," I said backing up. "There's no way I'm wearing that. And why do you even have that in your purse?"

"It's the darkest thing I have," Hattie said, smiling. "But it always gets the job done."

I threw my arms up, exasperated. There was no way I was squeezing into that thing.

"Does anyone else have anything Nikki can wear?" Grandma asked.

Greta looked in her purse and pulled out a sandwich bag with a neatly folded fabric inside. "I always keep an extra pair of underpants in my purse, but that's all I have."

"I have something," Irene said. "But it's lace . . ."

I grabbed the leopard-print bodysuit. "Fine! I'll go with this!"

I ducked back into the SUV and closed the door. Once the lights went off inside, I began the arduous task of squeezing into the bodysuit. Hattie was a tiny woman who clearly didn't have the same penchant for cinnamon rolls that I did. After much tugging and huffing and puffing, the bodysuit was on.

I stepped out of the van, and the grannies whistled.

"Oh stop it," I hissed. "Let's just get this over with."

I looked up and saw a girl, probably eleven or twelve years old, standing on the front porch. I looked over at Irene. "Are you going to introduce us to your friend?"

Hattie and Irene turned to see who was behind them.

"Oh shoot," Irene said. "Just act natural."

How natural could I act standing outside in a leopard-print bodysuit?

The girl came out to greet us. She had her hair pulled up in a bun and wore a long denim dress. "Miss Hattie, Miss Irene, I wondered where you went off to."

"We'll be back in the house soon, dear," Irene said sweetly. "We just need to talk to our friends for a minute."

The girl looked at me, and she blushed. I could tell she had lots of questions, but instead, she just smiled and walked back into the house.

"Okay," Irene said to us, "let's go."

"Not so fast," Grandma said, grabbing Irene's arm. "We're not going until you tell us what's going on with you two. Who lives here and what have you two been up to?"

Hattie and Irene looked at each other, and both finally sighed.

"Fine," Irene said. "The other day when you all

abandoned Hattie and me, we went to breakfast at this cute little country restaurant."

Hattie interrupted. "They had the best pancakes."

"Yes," Irene agreed. "They were very good. And while we were there, we sat next to these two well-dressed gentlemen. We smiled at them, they smiled at us, and the next thing you know, we were invited back to their house for pie."

Hattie winked. "And naturally, we thought pie meant . . ."

Grandma put her hand up to stop her. "I know what you thought it meant."

"Well," Irene said, "it turns out they actually meant pie. We followed them here and found out they are Mennonites. Samuel is widowed and lives with his daughter and their family."

"And Amos is his best friend," Hattie added. "He's widowed too. I got excited at first, thinking we could snag ourselves some religious guys, but they have some sort of code they live by."

"It's called morals, Hattie," Grandma interjected. "It's what most of us live by."

"Well, to be honest, I always thought morals were just skin-deep," Irene told us. "But these people, they're the real deal."

"We tried to trick them into thinking we were Mennonites too," Hattie said. "We even wore a little white thing on our heads the next day."

"The coffee filters," I said, rolling my eyes.

"Yeah, but they said we didn't have to wear one. Somehow, they knew right away we weren't one of them."

"Imagine that," Grandma smirked.

"After we realized we weren't going to seduce the men, we thought about leaving. But something strange happened. We started to like it here."

"They're so nice," Hattie said smiling. "They live such a happy, peaceful life, and we got sucked into it."

"Really?" Virginia asked, not convinced.

"Really," Irene said. "We're not saying we're joining the religion or anything, but something has been missing in our lives, and Hattie and I seemed to have found it here."

We were all quiet for a moment. I had never heard Irene talk like that before. When we started this trip, I never thought that Greta and Virginia would go boy crazy, and Hattie and Irene would find God.

"All right," Grandma finally said, "let's get this over with. Let's find the pony and get a hair sample, and then we'll leave you two with your new friends."

Hattie and Irene led us around the side of the house and through a gate that opened into the backyard.

"We need to hurry," Irene whispered. "We told Samuel and Amos we were coming outside to talk to you. If they get antsy, they'll come looking for us."

We tried to walk a little faster, but the only light we had was from the moon, so we were extra cautious as we made our way through their yard. Crickets chirped around us, and the air smelled like freshly mowed grass. The slight breeze rustled through the trees at the back of their property, and it reminded me so much of our farm in Illinois, I almost cried. Suddenly, I was homesick.

Greta let out a cry, and I turned to see what was wrong. A goat was nibbling on her shirt.

"Shoo!" she yelled, and instantly, the goat fell over onto its side.

"You killed it!" Hattie cried. "You killed the goat of a Mennonite!"

"It's not dead," Irene said. "It's one of those fainting goats little Emily was talking about."

The animal was stiff as a board for about ten seconds before it popped back up like nothing had happened. It skipped away, and Greta put her hand over her heart. "My stars, that thing scared me half to death."

We continued on through the field, staying close to the fence that separated the Mennonite's property from Kodiak's.

"We noticed a gate out here yesterday," Irene said. "It's over here somewhere."

We scanned the fence until we found the gate. Looking over into Kodiak's property, we could see a large barn. We paused for a minute and looked around. Everything was quiet.

"Let's get this over with," Grandma whispered.

We made our way to the barn, and we could hear

animals inside. We slipped in, and Grandma used the flashlight from her phone to light up the area. There was a cage along the left side of the barn, and two bright, beady eyes peeked out at us. A racoon stood on its hindlegs, holding onto the bars of its cage like a prisoner. It chattered at us, and Irene told it to be quiet. It got back down on all fours and crawled to the corner of its cage and started to eat something from a bowl, no longer interested in us.

Bales of hay lined the other side of the barn, and when Grandma shined her light on them, I noticed something right away.

"Wait," I whispered. "Shine your light over there again."

Grandma did, and I ran over and picked up a scarf that was draped across one of the bales. It was black with silver sequins sewn around the edges.

"That looks like the scarf Madison Paige wore during her performance," Greta said.

Grandma took it and looked it over. "What's it doing here?"

Hattie grabbed it and wrapped it around her neck. "The sequins are scratchy. How does she wear this thing?"

"Let's put it back," Grandma said. "We don't want to leave any trace that we were here. I don't see the pony, so it must be outside."

Hattie took off the scarf, and Grandma carefully put it back in its original position on the hay. As we walked out of the barn, Hattie looked over at the Mennonite farmhouse. It looked like every light was on, and it gave off a welcoming glow.

"I can't wait to get back there," said Hattie. "Did you know that they sing every evening, and then they have dessert? I bet they can make a good peach cobbler. Irene, remind me to ask them when we get back."

Just then, we heard a loud neigh come from the other side of the barn. We looked at each other, knowing we found our target.

We crept around the barn and saw the pony surrounded by a fence. We tried to open the gate, but it was locked.

"Climb in there," Grandma said, handing me a pair of scissors. "Cut a little off his tail."

"Don't let him kick you in the face," Hattie warned. "That happened to my cousin Steve, and he was cross-eyed for the rest of his life!"

Great. One more thing to worry about.

With a boost from Virginia, I went over the fence and made my way to the pony, who was standing at the back. I noticed he wasn't alone. There were two darker ponies and a few chickens loitering in the back with him.

I made my way toward them, scissors ready. Then I heard a noise that nearly stopped my heart. Was that a man talking?

"Get down!" Grandma whispered. "He's coming!"

Get down? Get down *where*? I ran to the back and

tried to hide between the ponies. A very curious chicken came over and pecked me on the head. I heard the grannies take off running, but I couldn't tell where they went.

I tried to shoo away the aggressive chicken, but for some reason, it was fascinated with my hair. I heard the barn door open, and then the voice of a woman filled the air.

"I'm pretty sure I left it in here." It was Madison's voice. "There it is. I'll just run in and grab it."

"Be careful," I heard Kodiak say to her. "I get some wild animals out here occasionally. Coyotes, bobcats . . . leopards."

I heard her laugh. "Leopards? I don't think they live in Missouri."

"You'd be surprised what shows up on my ranch."

Had I just been caught?

"Got it," Madison said when she came out of the barn. She laughed. "No leopards in there, thankfully!"

Through the pony's legs, I could see Kodiak standing by the gate, looking toward me. I held my breath, trying to stay as still as possible and hoping that the pony in front of me wouldn't move.

"That's good," he answered her. "For some reason they seem to like the ponies."

Shoot. I had definitely been caught.

They walked back up toward his house, and I stayed low until I heard the grannie's voices. I quickly snipped a few hairs from the pony's tail and got out of the pen as fast as I could.

"He caught me," I said as I handed the hair to Greta, and she slipped it into a sandwich bag and threw it into her purse.

"There's no way he could've seen you," Irene said. "Unless . . ."

We looked around and there, on the corner of the barn, was a camera. Hattie waved at it and blew it a kiss.

"Let's get out of here," Grandma said.

She didn't have to tell me twice. I took off running with the grannies following right behind me. I made it to the gate and burst onto the Mennonite's property, scaring four goats who fell over immediately.

I fell down next to them, completely out of breath. I might have been dressed like a leopard, but I definitely couldn't run like one.

"Can you imagine living like that?" Hattie asked. "Falling over and being paralyzed every time you got scared. And apparently it's contagious." She turned to look at Grandma. "How long do you think Nikki will be like that?"

"Oh, for heaven's sake," Grandma said, reaching down and taking my arm. She pulled me up. "You can catch your breath in the vehicle."

We made it to the SUV and said goodbye to Hattie and Irene. They went inside the farmhouse for some wholesome late-night singing while I picked straw out of my hair from the back seat. As we drove down the country road, headed toward town, my phone buzzed next to me. I picked it up. It was a text from Kodiak. I thought my heart was going to thump out of my chest as I read it. "I'll see you at the diner. We need to talk."

Yep, definitely busted.

"I CAN'T BELIEVE Hattie and Irene tried to seduce Mennonites," Grandma said on the way to the diner.

She pulled out her phone and brought up the picture of the horsehair that Archer Nash had sent her the day before. Greta handed her the bag of pony hair to see if it was a match.

Grandma Dean looked them over, then looked up at us, shaking her head. "I don't think it's the same. It looks like the pony hair is darker. What do you think?"

She handed them both to Greta, and Greta agreed.

I had my mind on other things. I didn't tell Grandma Dean that Kodiak had texted me and would be joining us that evening at the diner. By the time we got there, Willie, Billie, and Archer Nash were already sitting at their table in the back. To my dismay, Roxy was there too. Archer said something to her, and she threw her head back in laughter. She looked over at us then leaned in closer to Archer.

"She's way too young for him," Virginia scowled.

"He's a big boy," Grandma said calmly. "He can be with whoever he wants to be with."

"What if he wants to be with you?" I questioned.

Grandma ignored me and walked to the table, full of grace as usual. As we sat down, an awkwardness came over all of us, except for Greta and Willie.

Virginia leaned over to me and whispered. "Can you believe those two? Canoodling like that while we're trying to find Lou's killer." She looked over at Billie, and I could tell she didn't know if she could trust him or not. But even so, I could see she wanted to canoodle too.

A few minutes later Kodiak walked in and held the door open for Casius, who came in next on crutches. I couldn't help but smile when I saw him. He was dressed in his magician's outfit, cape and all. But that's not what made me chuckle. Even his crutches and cast were black.

I pulled a chair out for him at the far end of the table. "Wow, your medical gear matches your persona. Impressive."

He laughed dryly. "I always aim for impressive."

I took in a breath and smelled his cologne. It was deep and dark and made my heart skip a beat. Why did a good-smelling man do that?

Kodiak cleared his throat. "I see you got the hay out of your hair."

Casius looked at me, confused, then back up at Kodiak. I could tell his mind was going somewhere it didn't need to go.

"It's not what you think," I whispered as I sat down next to Casius. I was surprised when he looked relieved.

Kodiak sat down on the other side of Casius but leaned across him to talk to me. "I have cameras on my property," he said, his voice low and angry.

"I realize that now," I answered, trying to stay as calm as possible.

"What were you doing snooping around? And you looked ridiculous in that leopard outfit!"

That was a low blow.

"Leopard outfit? What are you guys talking about?" Casius asked.

"Oh yeah?" I angrily whispered back. "And what were you and Madison Paige doing in your barn that she had to come back later and retrieve some of her clothing?!"

"What?" Casius practically yelled. The whole table turned to look at us, and Grandma gave me a death stare from across the table.

Kodiak got up and walked over to Greta's purse, which was slung over the back of the chair. "I want to know why you have this!" He reached into Greta's purse and pulled out a sandwich bag. Unfortunately for him, it wasn't the bag of pony hair.

"My underpants!" Greta shrieked. She snatched the bag from him, and Willie got up, knocking over his chair behind him.

"How dare you expose her bloomers!" he yelled at Kodiak. "I'll give you a real reason to wear that eyepatch!" He swung wildly and punched Kodiak in the face, sending him sideways into a nearby table.

When Kodiak steadied himself, I was sure he was going to slug Willie back, but instead, he straightened out his shirt and wiped the blood from his nose. He looked at me, frustration in his eyes, and stormed out, grabbing a stack of napkins on his way.

I got up to follow him, and Casius stood up too. "You're not leaving me behind. Not with this group."

I helped him up, and we went as fast as we could to the door, which wasn't nearly fast enough for me, but pretty fast for a guy on crutches. Thankfully, Kodiak was still sitting in his truck by the time we made it. I opened the door and climbed in.

"Kodiak, I'm sorry. Are you okay?"

He pulled down the mirror and looked at his nose. "I don't think it's broken."

I could tell that the non-patched eye was already swelling and bruising.

I helped Casius into the truck, and then I explained the whole thing to both of them.

"So, you think I'm the killer?" Kodiak asked. "You

think I would be capable of doing that to another human being? Me, who rescues animals and takes care of them for a living? Have I not proven that I value life?"

"I'm sorry," I apologized again. "If it makes you feel any better, I don't think that anymore. The pony hair didn't match the horsehair found at the scene of the crime."

"Of course it didn't," he said angrily. "Because I'm not a murderer. And what about him?" He pointed to Casius.

Casius looked shocked. "What *about* me?!"

Kodiak narrowed his eyes at him. "You're the one who swindled Lou out of a bunch of money. That's why Billie can't stand you. You got the title 'liar and a thief' for a reason!"

It was Casius' turn to get angry now. "I'm a lot of things, but a liar and a thief aren't among them!"

"Well, then tell us what happened." I said to him. "Why does everyone think you are?"

Casius leaned back in the seat and exhaled. "Fine." He took another slow breath, then continued. "Six or seven years ago someone was selling a bunch of property on the outskirts of Branson. They were selling lots for a hundred thousand dollars apiece. I heard from a realtor buddy of mine that we could buy these lots and make a huge profit. Branson was expanding, and not only were more and more people visiting the area each year, but more and more people were moving here. It looked like a huge investment opportunity. The only thing was, I didn't have a lot of cash. I had saved up enough to buy one of these lots, but I wanted to buy the whole block. I talked to Willie, and he was in. We would put our money together, and I planned to use my connections with my realtor buddy to get us a good price when we sold it."

"So, what happened?" I asked. "Did you sell it?"

"Ha!" Kodiak scoffed. "He pulled the old magician act and made all of Lou's money disappear!"

Casius scowled at him. "I didn't do that. The lots never sold. They sat there for years, and we kept dropping the price. They're still for sale."

"How much are they now?" I asked.

Casius rubbed his temples. "Fifteen grand apiece."

"Ouch," I said, cringing. "That's rough."

"So maybe you killed Lou so you could sell the land and at least make your money back by the time all the lots sold," Kodiak pointed out.

I looked at Casius, waiting for an answer. That seemed plausible to me.

He looked up at us, and there was a sadness in his eyes. "I felt so bad that things went south. Lou had a lot more to lose than I did. That was his retirement. It took me until earlier this year, but I bought him out. I gave him back every dime he put into it. I'm basically broke now, but at least I'm guilt-free."

"Oh man," Kodiak said, leaning toward him. "I'm so sorry. Why didn't you tell the guys?"

Casius huffed. "Billie hated me long before that. I'm never going to convince him I'm not the guy he thinks I am."

We sat there quietly for a moment, then Casius leaned forward again. "So, what's going on with you and Madison Paige?"

"Yeah," I said, looking at Kodiak. "And why weren't you doing your show tonight?"

He looked at me and rolled his eyes. "I do a matinee on Sundays, but I take the evening off. And Madison and I have kind of been seeing each other a little here and there. It's hard to find someone when you're an entertainer. Women have a hard time seeing me as something other than the Kodiak King."

"I hear you," Casius sighed. "Good for you, man. I hope it works out. She seems like a nice girl."

Kodiak smiled. "She is. She's a lot of fun too."

I nudged him in the arm. "But does she dress up in a leopard outfit and hide out with your pony?"

He pulled a piece of hay out of my hair. "Thankfully, no."

"Well," I sighed, "I guess I should get back in there. You guys coming?"

Kodiak shook his head. "I don't feel like dealing with Willie. I'll give him a call tomorrow and straighten out this whole mess. But for now, I'll let him cool down."

I looked at Casius. "What about you?"

"He's my ride," he nodded toward Kodiak. "Besides, I've had enough excitement for one night."

He climbed out of the truck so I could get out, and as I helped him back in, I took in another deep breath of his cologne. I was sure I had just breathed in a thousand cancer-causing chemicals, but I didn't care—it was intoxicating.

Casius caught me and smiled. He leaned forward and whispered in my ear. "Remember, I aim to be impressive." He leaned back in the truck, and I closed the door.

I stared at him for a moment, taking in his perfectly chiseled features and his five o'clock shadow that seemed to add to his darkness, and I didn't doubt him one bit.

THE NEXT MORNING, I woke up to the noise of Grandma's hairdryer. Even with the bathroom door closed, it still sounded like she was standing right next to me. I looked over at the alarm – seven o'clock. Too early to be awake, in my opinion.

She opened the bathroom door, and a burst of light filled the room. "Good! You're up!" she said cheerfully. "Virginia and Greta are meeting us in the lobby in thirty minutes. We're going out for breakfast." She tossed me some clothes. "I already picked out your outfit for the day."

Well, that was that. Apparently, I was joining them for breakfast. Maybe we'd go to that restaurant Hattie and Irene told us about—the one with the pancakes. Did she ever tell us what restaurant that was?

Grandma was back in the bathroom getting ready, and I joined her at the counter. We put on our makeup side by side, and I was completely finished before she had even started on her eyes.

She handed me a bottle and told me to spritz my hair. "Honestly, Nikki, what are you going to do when you move out, and I'm not there to guide you each morning?"

Move out? I hadn't thought of leaving in months.

Soon we were ready and headed to the lobby. We walked in and were surprised to see that not only were Greta and Virginia there, but Hattie and Irene as well.

"What are you two doing here?" Grandma asked them.

Irene shrugged. "We thought we'd join you for breakfast today." She looked over at Virginia, and it looked like they shared some kind of secret signal back and forth.

"And maybe," Virginia said, "we'll stop by and see Thomas after."

"Oh no." Grandma said. "I can't even think about that right now. I have too much on my mind with Lou's death. Maybe once we get all that straightened out, I can think about visiting Thomas."

Greta put her hand on Grandma's arm. "Geraldine, we know you're afraid . . ."

Grandma was offended. "I'm not afraid, Greta. We are neck deep in this mess, and until we get it figured out, I'm not going to walk into another mess. Now, who's coming to breakfast with me?"

She turned and walked out of the lobby, leaving the rest of us standing there watching her go.

Greta sighed. "I don't blame her for being afraid. Coming face-to-face with your past isn't an easy thing."

"Well," Irene said, "we better head out there before she leaves without us."

Virginia dangled her keys. "She won't get too far without these."

Minutes later, we were all buckled in and headed to the restaurant where Hattie and Irene had met their Mennonite friends. It was on the edge of town in a cute, country-style building. I could smell the sweet smell of sausage and syrup as soon as I got out. I inhaled the scent. It was heavenly.

Once we were seated, Hattie and Irene asked about the pony hair from the night before.

"It didn't match," Greta said. I could tell she was disappointed. "We haven't had one thing pan out for us in this investigation. It seems like everything leads to a dead end."

Virginia stirred creamer into her coffee. "Nikki, tell Hattie and Irene what you told us last night on the way home from the diner."

I filled them in on the reason why Billie didn't like Casius and also what little I knew about Madison and Kodiak. "So, I think we can safely scratch both of them off our list."

Virginia pulled the suspect list out of her purse and put a line through their names. "So, that leaves Archer and Billie." Grandma and Virginia looked at each other, silently daring the other one to say something about their guys. Neither one spoke.

I decided to try to change the subject a little. "Virginia, Greta, did you two ever learn anything about a family dispute?"

"Not much," Greta answered. "Just that Billie and Lou were usually at odds with each other. Apparently, they argued quite a bit."

Virginia got defensive. "But brothers fight. That doesn't mean they go off and kill each other."

The waitress came over smiling, carrying a large tray loaded up with our food. I was so thankful pancakes had come to our rescue. Once everyone got some sugar and carbs into their system, the mood lightened at the table.

"We passed the Butterfly Museum on the way here," Greta said. "I would love to go there."

"I would too!" Virginia said. "Let's try to fit that in before we leave."

Grandma's phone rang, and she quietly answered it while the rest of us talked about places we still wanted to visit while we were in town.

When Grandma put her phone down, I looked over at her and saw that she was nearly white as a ghost.

"Grandma, are you okay?" Who was that?"

Everyone at the table looked at her, alarmed.

"What's going on?" Greta asked, panic in her voice.

Grandma stared blankly at us for a minute, then

collected herself. "It was Archer. Billie has been arrested . . . for murder."

"What?!" we all gasped.

Virginia was in shock, and Greta and Irene both put their arms around her to comfort her. I didn't think she was breathing, so I said her name and reminded her to take a breath.

"What evidence do they have?" Irene asked Grandma.

"I don't know," Grandma answered. "Archer said to meet him at the theater, and he'd tell us everything he knows."

She waved the waitress over and told her we needed our bill right away. Thankfully, the waitress had it ready, and she slipped it out of her apron and put it on the table. Grandma didn't even look at it. She just handed the waitress her debit card and told her we needed to leave right away. The waitress scurried off, and Greta and Irene helped Virginia to her feet. She was in tears now, and the rest of us were still in shock.

Willie met us in front of Archer's theater and took us inside to Archer's dressing room. He was just getting off the phone when we walked in.

"What's going on?" Grandma asked him. "Why was Billie arrested?"

"It's not looking good for him," Archer said. "Someone called the police and told them to check Billie's dressing room. The police showed up early this morning and found a half-empty bottle of antifreeze in a box in the closet.

Poor Willie was wringing his hands. "He had to have been set up. You believe that, right, Archer? You know Billie never would've killed Lou."

Archer rubbed his forehead. "I'm not sure what to think."

"Billie wouldn't do that!" Willie cried. "Billie wouldn't sabotage our own show!"

"Well, who would? Who would gain from taking you guys out?" Grandma asked.

"Anybody who wants to open for the hottest show in Branson!" Willie yelled. "I think someone wants our show!"

We all looked at Archer.

"Could that be true?" Grandma asked. "Is someone trying to steal the show out from under them?"

Archer looked exhausted. "I guess it's possible. Why else would someone kill Lou?"

"Well," Greta said slowly, "you know he was making some promises to young women. Maybe one of them retaliated."

"What kind of promises?" Willie asked.

Greta told them about her conversation with Amy's drummer, and Willie and Archer looked shocked.

Archer stood up, angry at the news. "I've been telling the group they should hire a woman to cater to the men in the audience. But I had no idea that Lou was interviewing women and putting them in that kind of position." He looked at Willie. "Did you know?"

"Heck no!" Willie answered. "You know we didn't want a woman in the group. They'd be nothin' but trouble!" He looked at us and his cheeks flushed. "No offense, ladies."

"None taken," Hattie smiled. "Some of us take pride in the trouble we cause."

"This . . . Amy . . . you talked to," Archer said. "Do you think she had anything to do with it?"

"We can't rule her out," Grandma answered. "But our gut says she didn't do it."

"We need to find out who all Lou talked to," Archer said, heading to the door. Then he stopped and spun around. "What am I going to do tonight? I don't have a preshow. Willie, Billie, and Lou are now just Willie."

"We can do it," Greta offered. "Geraldine used to be a performer. I'm sure she still has some pizazz in her, and the rest of us can help."

"Oh no," Grandma said, shaking her head. "I gave that up a long time ago."

"I can help you," Willie said. "It's just nine in the morning. We have all day to put something together."

I looked around the room, terrified, expecting to see the same faces on the other grannies. But instead, they were nodding. How could Willie put a show together in less than a day with this group? With me? Surely, they wouldn't need me. I would just sit on the side and cheer them on.

"Come on, Geraldine. What do you say?" Virginia asked.

Archer looked at Grandma. "Are you up for it?"

In my mind, I pleaded with Grandma Dean. *Say no! Say no!*

She took a deep breath. "Well, if it will help you out . . ."

Archer nodded to Willie. "Willie, you work with the ladies and come up with a show. I'm going to see if I can figure out who Lou had been talking to."

Willie snapped into action. "Okay!" he said. "Which one of you ladies can play an instrument?"

Hattie raised her hand. "Fifty years ago, I played the piccolo!"

Oh boy. This was going to be interesting.

18

"Okay . . ." Willie said slowly. "What else can you gals do?"

Irene stepped forward. "Hattie and I have been singing hymns *a cappella* with a Mennonite family the last few days. Maybe the two of us could sing a few."

"Great!" Willie said, excited. "Our conservative crowd will love that! Can you two go practice with them, put together a few songs, and then be back here after lunch?"

Hattie and Irene said they would and took off with Virginia's keys. Willie turned to look at Greta, Virginia, and me. "What about you three. What do you do for a living?"

Greta smiled. "I'm a writer. I write a Christian sex education curriculum for schools. Virginia is a wedding planner, and Nikki is a serial bride."

"Great!" Willie announced. "You three will do some

comedy sketches. That has to be comedy gold right there." He looked around for a minute. "You gals can work here in Archer's dressing room. Geraldine and I will take the big stage."

Willie and Grandma Dean left the room, and I stared at Greta and Virginia, hoping they would take charge. Thankfully, they did.

Virginia pulled her notebook from her purse and handed it to me. "Okay, let's all brainstorm. Nikki, you write everything down."

I sat down at Archer's vanity, and Greta handed me a pen. Greta suddenly laughed. "It *is* pretty funny, isn't it?"

"What?" I asked.

"That a sex education writer, a wedding planner, and a serial bride have all crossed paths like this. It's like our Creator brought us all together to write this sketch."

Virginia chuckled. "Well, our Creator is either a genius or has one heck of a sense of humor."

Greta smiled. "I think it's both."

"Wait," I said, pen ready. "Can we use that? Should I write that down?"

"Sure," Greta said. "Jot that down." She thought for a minute. "I've never really written anything funny. Have you, Virginia?"

Virginia shook her head. "Not really." She grabbed her head like she was dizzy. "How is it that we're the ones writing this, and Hattie and Irene are singing hymns? It's like the world is upside-down in Branson."

I had thought that same thing myself.

"Think . . . think . . ." Greta told herself. Then she had an idea. "What if we came up with some jokes about each of us and then incorporated that into a little sketch? We can do it like Willie and Billie did it. We can set each other up for our jokes."

"Okay," I said, pen poised in the air. "Like what?"

Greta bit her lip and thought for a moment more. "Okay! I got it! Virginia, you could come up to me and say, 'Hey Greta, what do you think about sex on TV?' and I could answer, 'Seems a bit dangerous. What if you fall off?!'"

She laughed at her joke, and that made Virginia and I laugh.

"We've been spending too much time with Lloyd," I said as I wrote down the joke.

"We'll ask Willie if that's too racy for the crowd," Virginia said. "But let's keep on writing!"

Greta's joke had gotten us started, and soon, we were coming up with jokes one right after the other. We didn't know if they were any good, but they sure made us laugh. I wrote down another one and then flipped the paper over to write some more.

"Shoot!" I said, turning to face them. "We're out of paper."

"Well, poop," Greta said. "My notebook is in Virginia's vehicle which is with the other girls."

"We're almost done," I said, turning back around. "Surely there's a piece of paper around here somewhere."

I opened a drawer in Archer's vanity. "Here's one!" I said, pulling it out.

I started to write on it, and Virginia stopped me. "Wait! I think something is written on the other side."

I flipped it over and saw the hot-pink, feminine handwriting. "It's a note from Roxy to Archer." I started reading it out loud.

"Dear Archer, I've sat down to write this a hundred times, but I don't know what to say. Part of me wants to say that we broke it off months ago, and what we had was never that serious to begin with. I can date whoever I want, just like you can date whoever you want. But part of me feels like I should apologize. I'm sure seeing me with Lou the other night wasn't easy. I had my reasons for being with him, but I'm sure they'll just feel like excuses to you. Maybe one day, we can sit down and talk about this, but for now, just know that I made a mistake. Lou and I are over. He's been making promises he can't keep, and I'm going to put a stop to it. I hope you and I can still be friends. I don't want to lose what we have. Love, Roxy XOXO"

I looked up at Greta and Virginia. "Put a stop to it? What do you think that means?"

"Hand me that notebook," Virginia said to me. "I think we have another suspect."

I looked at the time. "It's nearly noon. Should we go

grab a quick lunch and see if we can pay Roxy a little visit?"

Virginia looked determined. "Let's go. Maybe we can bust her and clear Billie's name before the show tonight."

I silently prayed that was possible. The last thing I wanted to do was get on that stage. Especially if there was someone out there intent on taking anyone out who performed on it.

19

"PULL AROUND THE BACK," Greta told the Uber driver as we pulled into the parking lot of Roxy's theater. "Maybe there's a back door we can sneak into," she whispered to us.

As he drove around the backside of the building, I noticed a loading dock with a door next to it. Virginia and Greta saw it too.

"Just drop us off here," Virginia told the driver.

Once the car was out of sight, I tried the back door, but it was locked. I decided to climb up onto the loading dock and try that door. To my relief, it came right open. I ran around and unlocked the regular door for Virginia and Greta. Once we were all inside, we made our way through the halls, looking for Roxy's dressing room.

The theater was already alive with workers. Since it

was a dinner theater, the staff was already busy in the kitchen prepping the evening's meal.

"I saw her car out front, so I'm sure she's here," Virginia said.

"How do you know it was her car?" I asked.

"There was a hot pink car with the license plates ILUV80S. I assume that belongs to her."

We walked past an unmarked door, and we all stopped when we heard singing.

"I think that's her," Greta mouthed.

Virginia knocked on the door, and the singing stopped. A woman with short blond hair opened the door.

"Oh, I'm sorry," Virginia said. "We were looking for someone. I'm sorry we bothered you."

The woman looked familiar, and a sly smile rose on her face. "Who are you looking for?"

Greta started to answer it, and then it hit me. "Roxy?" I asked.

She smiled even wider. "Didn't recognize me without my wig, did you?"

Virginia's mouth was wide open. "You look completely different!"

Roxy laughed and invited us in. "How did you guys even get in here?"

"We snuck in the back," I admitted.

She laughed again and motioned for us to sit down. We all sat down on one of her black, leather couches, moving hot-pink, furry pillows out of the way first.

Roxy took a seat on the couch across from us. "So, what can I do for you ladies? I'm guessing you're not here for tickets to my show."

Virginia was in no mood for small talk, so she got right to it. "We want to know what happened between you and Lou."

Roxy leaned over and picked up a bottle of alcohol from a tray in the middle of the coffee table between us. She slowly poured the amber liquid into her glass, then gave it a swirl. "And why should I tell you?"

Virginia stood up, fists clenched, and Greta and I pulled her back down to the couch.

"My friend is a bit emotional," Greta said to Roxy. "You know that Billie was arrested this morning . . ."

Roxy stopped her. "Wait, what? I didn't hear that." Now we had her full attention.

"He was arrested for Lou's murder," I added. "But we don't think he's guilty."

Roxy's jaw flinched. I didn't know if she was angry or fighting back tears or both.

"We just want to know about your relationship with Lou," I continued.

"No," Roxy said. "You want to know if I killed him."

The room went silent.

"Well," Greta said. "Did you?"

"You three think you can break into my theater and then accuse me of murder?" Roxy was not happy.

"We read the note you wrote to Archer. You told him you were going to put a stop to whatever Lou was doing. We want to know what that was," Virginia said.

Now Roxy was furious. "AND you read my personal letter to Archer? Does he know you did that?"

This was not going well. We weren't going to get any answers like this. This would be a good time for Greta to pull out some tasty treat from her purse and pass it to Roxy, but instead, she had her hands full, holding Virginia back. My mind raced. Could I pull off the snack trick? Did I even have a snack in my purse?

I remembered I had some caramels in there that I had picked up from the gift shop at the zip line place. I reached in my purse and felt around. There it was! "Here," I said pulling out a caramel. "Would you like this?"

As I stretched out my hand toward her, I saw the look of disgust on her face, and then I saw what I was holding. My caramel had come out of the wrapper on one side and was stuck to a tampon.

I pulled it off and tried to hand it to her, but she looked at me like I was crazy. Which I was. Obviously, that trick didn't work if you were under the age of sixty or if you frequently left your purse in the car on warm days.

Greta leaned forward and grabbed a bottle of alcohol from the table. "May I?"

Roxy sighed. "Why not."

Greta poured herself a drink and took a long,

drawn-out sip. "Look," she said to Roxy. "We're in deep on this one. We didn't mean to get here, but we are."

Suddenly, Greta reminded me of a mob boss, sitting there staring at Roxy. And was that a hint of an accent I detected? "We don't want anyone else to get hurt, if you know what I mean."

I looked up at Roxy to see if she was buying Greta's mobster act. She had to think we were nuts. I just tried to give her a caramel tampon and now this.

Roxy sighed and leaned back in her chair. "I don't want anyone else to get hurt either. What do you want to know?"

Greta took another sip, but otherwise didn't move. She narrowed her eyes, and yep, when she spoke, there was definitely an accent. "We just want to know what you know."

Roxy was hesitant but finally spoke. "Lou walked me out to my car a couple of weeks ago. We had been at the diner after a show, and he was always coming on to me, so him following me out to my car was nothing new. But then he said something to me he had never said before."

"What was that?" I asked. Greta gave me a death stare. Clearly, she was running the show here.

"He told me that if I went on a date with him, he could get me in their show."

"Why would you be interested in that offer?" Virginia asked. "You have your own show. Wouldn't that be a step down?"

"Opening the show for the hottest guy in Branson?" Roxy scoffed. "I'd take that any day. For two years, I've tried to get Archer to talk to the guys and let me in on their little show."

"Why would you give up your own show?" I asked her.

Roxy went quiet, then slowly got up and walked to her dressing table. She opened a drawer and took out a paper. She handed it to Virginia. "Take a look at my numbers. My audience is dwindling. I get this printout every month, and every month it looks worse. I'm tired of the stress, the pressure of trying to keep things fresh and new. I sing eighties songs, for goodness sake. How fresh and new can you make something that is almost forty years old?"

Greta gasped and broke character. "The eighties were almost forty years ago?!" She collected herself and narrowed her eyes again.

Roxy went on. "I know it was wrong, but I thought maybe Lou was my way in. So, I went on a date with him."

"Just one date?" I asked.

"No, several. He kept telling me he was talking to the guys, and things were looking good. I thought I had a real chance. And then one afternoon, I was driving by Archer's theater and saw Lou's truck out there. I don't know what made me stop. But for some reason, I did. I walked into the theater and was surprised to see a woman standing on the stage singing. I hung back to

145

see what was going on. When she stopped, Lou clapped for her like he clapped for me every time I would sing to him. Then he said something that made me sick. He told her that if she went on a date with him, and the others thought they were serious, they would be more likely to let her into the group. That dirty scoundrel was just using his position to get women."

"So, what'd you do about it?" Greta asked, her accent getting thicker.

"I confronted him after the woman left. I told him that he was just using her. That she was trying to move up the Branson ladder, and he was taking advantage of her. He didn't even deny it." She plopped back down on the couch across from us. "I felt like such a sucker. By that time, Archer had already seen us kissing at the diner by the bathroom, and he wasn't talking to me . . . I just felt like I had lost any chance I had to actually get in the group."

"So, you wrote Archer the letter apologizing, and then what? How were you going to put a stop to Lou?" I asked.

"I told Lou that I was going to tell Archer what he was up to. See, Lou was always worried about losing his position in the group anyway. He's not actually Willie and Billie's brother."

"He's not?" we all gasped.

"No, he's their cousin. Willie and Billie started the group a long time ago and were popular long before they hired Lou. And Lou was always paranoid that they were going to cut him out one day. I think he thought that if he was able to con a woman into dating him, and then he got her in the group, she would always feel like she owed him something and wouldn't vote him out if the brothers actually took it to a vote. He wanted an ally, or at least, someone else lower on the totem pole."

She looked at us and rolled her eyes. "And before you ask again, no, I didn't kill him."

"You had a motive," I said to her. "And no one would even think twice about you being back in their dressing rooms since you always hung out together."

"I'm trying to make my life less stressful," she scoffed. "Murdering someone is not less stressful. Besides, Archer can pull a lot of strings in this town. I need to be on his good side. Killing one of his friends isn't going to get me there. Plus, I'm not the kind of person who just goes around knocking off people who do me wrong. I'd have one heck of a hit list."

"Tell me about it," Greta said, still keeping up her act.

Virginia burst into tears. "If you're innocent, then how are we going to free Billie?"

"I told you what I know," Roxy said. "Now you tell me what *you* know. Maybe I can help connect the dots."

We told her about the applesauce and antifreeze and about what was found in Billie's room in a box. And how someone had tipped the cops off and told them where to look. "And there was a blond horsehair in his hand." I added.

"Horsehair? Willie is terrified of horses. The only person I know who has horses is Kodiak, and I think they are actually ponies."

"They are," I confirmed. "And we checked last night, and they weren't a match."

"So," Roxy said, thinking, "Lou is dead, and Billie is framed. Did anyone try to do anything to Willie?"

"Not yet," I answered.

"It seems like someone wants their show," she said. "And they want it bad enough that they don't care who they hurt or kill to get it. Whoever did this knew Lou's routine. They knew he took his medication every night after the show, and he put it in his applesauce."

"Medication?" I asked. "That's why he ate applesauce every evening?"

"It has to be someone in his inner circle," Virginia said. "Someone who knew he ate it every night and would be able to get into the theater."

"You ladies saw how easy it was to get in during the day. The front doors are always locked, but people are in and out of the back all the time," Roxy pointed out. Then her eyes opened wide. "What if it was one of the women Lou was stringing along? Maybe he told her about the applesauce or it came up in conversation one day. She could've snuck it into his dressing room."

"But who would do that?" I asked.

Roxy shrugged. "It could be anyone trying to rise through the ranks here."

I looked at Greta and Virginia, and they looked back at me, sadness in their eyes.

Greta dropped her mobster accent. "Who did you see on stage that night you walked in?"

Roxy shrugged again. "I had never seen her before. But she had the voice of an angel. She had a lot to learn about performing, though. She reminded me of a much younger version of myself."

"Amy," I said quietly.

Greta pulled one of her flyers out from her purse. "Is this her?"

Roxy took it and studied it for a minute. "No, that's not her."

We breathed a sigh of relief. But clearly, Lou had been making promises to a lot of women. Who knew how many?

My phone buzzed in my pocket, and when I pulled it out, I saw I had a text. "It's Grandma Dean," I told them. "She said she and Willie are ready for us, and Hattie and Irene are on their way."

We stood up and thanked Roxy for her time and promised her we would keep her in the loop. As I started toward the door, she grabbed my arm. I looked up at her, surprised.

"Your grandma is one lucky lady," she said to me.

"What do you mean?" I asked.

"Archer has really fallen for her, which is strange because usually, he likes younger women. But he told me the other night that this is different. That there's something special about her."

I didn't know what to say. They had only known each other for a short time, but I noticed the connection too.

Roxy released my arm. "I hope it works out for them," she said. "I really do. Archer is an amazing man, and he deserves to be happy. Your grandma seems amazing too."

"She is," I said to her, "and she isn't someone to mess with."

Roxy laughed. "Noted."

We walked out of the theater, and I felt anxiety grip my chest. It was showtime. Or at least, rehearsal for the showtime.

As another Uber driver took us back to the theater, Greta turned around in the front seat and looked at me.

"I appreciate what you tried to do back there with the caramel. But next time, leave the advanced interrogation techniques to me."

When we arrived back at Archer's theater, we saw Hattie and Irene walking up to the door. We got out and followed them in. I had never heard them sing before and was curious to see if they could pull it off. I was equally curious to see if Greta, Virginia, and I could do the same thing.

We opened the door to the big theater, and I froze, my heart stopping in my chest. There, on the stage, was Willie playing the guitar, and Grandma singing. She beamed brightly as she bopped along beside him. She was a natural. Suddenly, it hit me. I had never seen her perform before.

The other grannies gasped beside me. Greta leaned over to me. "She doesn't even sing in church anymore. When she gave up singing, she really gave it up."

Irene laughed. "She's going to be hoarse tomorrow."

When they finished their song, Willie waved us over. "Let's do our blocking on our stage since that's where we'll be performing. That way, it will make more sense to you gals tonight."

We followed him back out of the big theater and into the room where we would be performing. He asked us about our ideas, and we each told him what we had.

"Perfect!" he said. "We'll call this 'Willie's Variety Hour'!"

We got to work and, hours later, we were as ready as we were going to be. The costume department had lined up country dresses for us to wear—each one frilly and in a different color, complete with cowboy boots. Hattie didn't have hers on for five minutes before she was saying she wanted to eat a steak.

Finally, the hour arrived. I went over and over in my head what I needed to do and when I needed to do it. I couldn't believe I was about to perform in front of so many people. I looked at the grannies as we all stood in the hallway outside the dressing rooms. There was a nervous excitement buzzing around them. Even

Virginia, who had been melancholy all day, was smiling.

Willie disappeared for a minute, then came back. "We've got a full house tonight! You ladies ready?"

I wanted to say no and take off running out of the building, but Grandma took my hand and smiled at me. "You're going to be great," she whispered.

"Thanks," I said back. "You are too. And it's an honor to share the stage with you."

Grandma got tears in her eyes. "I never thought I'd be on a stage again. It's even more special that you're here with me."

Just like that, my anxiety left me. Instead of feeling full of fear and dread, I felt thankful. This was one of the biggest blessings I'd had so far in my life. Not that I was going on stage to perform for the first time ever, but that I was doing it with Grandma Dean—world traveler, a one-time European superstar, and the woman who had turned into my best friend.

I stepped out on the stage and took in the lights and the applause. This was it. And I was ready.

We started off the show with a song that Willie had taught us. We sang and did our simple little dance routine. Then he and Grandma did a duet which was beautiful. Next up were Hattie and Irene. They had blown us away during the rehearsal, and somehow, they were even better now. I don't know how those Mennonites did it, maybe it was a true act of God, but they had somehow taught two crazy ladies how to praise *a cappella* style, and to do it like professionals.

After two hymns from them, Virginia, Greta, and I were up. We walked to the front of the stage and did a little skit on married versus single women. Then we got ready for our last joke.

Virginia frowned and looked at her body, then looked over at mine. "Why is it that married women are heavier than single women?" Greta laughed. "Because a single woman goes home, looks in the fridge, then goes to bed. But a married woman sees what's in bed and goes to the fridge."

The crowd laughed at our jokes, and we took our places at the back of the stage, getting ready for the next song we were all going to sing. Thankfully, it was one we all knew, so it was easy to clap along and not worry we were going to mess something up. And that's how our hour went. A song we all sang, then a duet with Grandma and Willie, a hymn or two from Hattie and Irene and a skit from Virginia, me, and Greta.

It went by so fast, and I couldn't believe it when it was over.

We took our bows, and I absorbed all of the applause. Grandma took my hand and squeezed it. This had been the best night of my life.

21

WE SAT AT THE DINER, and all lifted up our root beer floats.

"To Branson's newest performers," Archer said.

We lifted our glasses and then took a swig. Roxy sat across from us and smiled. "I heard you guys did great! I'm proud of you."

Grandma looked at me, surprised. We filled her in on the ride over about our conversation with Roxy, but none of us really expected this change in attitude toward us. If anything, I thought maybe she'd be upset we had stolen the show for the night. But maybe that's why she wasn't upset—she knew it was just for the night.

Kodiak and Casius came in late, and I was happy to see them. I pulled out a chair for Casius and took his crutches so he could sit down.

"I was starting to wonder if you were going to make it," I said to him.

He laughed. "I was starting to wonder too. Kodiak came by and picked me up after my show, and we swung by and saw Madison Paige after the Seven Sven show got out. I had to sit there and endure those two making out before I finally got Kodiak to let her go."

"Ah, young love." Roxy smiled.

"It makes me sick," Casius grumbled.

"Oh, come on," I said, nudging him. "You're jealous, and you know it."

He gave me a look that made my stomach do a flip-flop. "Maybe I am."

Kodiak was still standing at the head of the table, and he reached over to pat Grandma on the back. "I heard you gals tore up the stage tonight!"

"They were amazing!" Willie gushed. "I was real proud of them. Real proud for sure."

Everyone moved over so Kodiak had room to sit, and he took a seat next to Hattie, who was thrilled to have him sit by her. Virginia, however, looked far from thrilled.

"Are you okay, Virginia?" I asked.

She looked up at me, sadness in her eyes. "I feel so bad for Billie. I wish he was here celebrating with us."

The table was suddenly silent, all the excitement and energy sucked out when we were brought back to reality.

"I think we should all have a discussion," Roxy said.

"Lay it all out on the table. Let's talk about what we know. Maybe if we work together, we can come up with something. We loved Lou together, and we can work together to figure out who killed him."

I thought that was a good idea, and judging by the nods around the table, I think everyone did.

"Ok," Grandma said. "This is what we know . . ."

Between her and Archer, they explained the little evidence the police had. The grannies and I explained our trip to Kodiak's ranch, and Roxy shared why she dated Lou. It was the first time Archer had heard the whole story, and I could tell he was upset, but he managed to keep his emotions at bay.

"The missing key is this—who knew about the applesauce? Who knew he put his medication in it every night and took it without fail?"

The group was quiet for a moment.

"We all teased him about not swallowing pills," Casius finally said. "And we did it all the time. The guy couldn't even take a Tylenol without having to crush it and put it in something. Anyone could've heard us teasing him."

"That's true," Kodiak said. "The man could swallow oysters whole and drink down a bottle of whiskey in three giant gulps, but you couldn't ask him to swallow a pill. We gave him a lot of flak for that."

Everyone went silent again.

"So, are we still having a little memorial service

tomorrow afternoon at your theater?" Roxy asked Archer.

Archer looked around the table. "Should we still do it?"

"Why wouldn't we?" Casius asked.

"Well," Archer answered. "We've uncovered some unsavory things about him. Should we still move forward with it?"

"You're probably going to uncover some unsavory things about me when I'm gone too," Roxy admitted.

"We've all got skeletons in our closets," Casius said. "He was our friend. I think we should do it."

"If not for him, then for us," Roxy added. "It's our way of letting him go."

"Okay, then," Archer said. "It's still on."

"I have a song to sing," Roxy said. "What about you guys?"

Archer looked at Grandma. "Would you like to sing something with me?"

Grandma laughed. "If I still have a voice tomorrow, I'd love to."

Kodiak put his arm around Hattie, and she giggled.

"I heard you're quite the entertainer," he teased. "Are you going to sing something too?"

"Maybe Irene and I could come up with something." She smiled. Then she sighed. "You know, we're going to be leaving soon, and I still haven't gotten my dang peach cobbler. I've been craving it since we got here."

Kodiak started telling her about a restaurant in

town that had the best cobbler, and suddenly, Grandma leaned forward. "Hattie, hug Kodiak."

We all looked at Grandma like she was crazy.

Hattie didn't need to be told twice, and she threw her arms around the big, burly man.

Kodiak laughed. "What's going on?"

"Okay, Hattie . . ." Grandma said. "Hattie, let go!"

Hattie pulled away, and Kodiak had to adjust his shirt

"Does that make you want to eat anything?" Grandma asked.

Grandma got more crazy looks from us, and Hattie looked up at her and smiled. "Peach cobbler."

"And do you remember exactly when you first started craving peach cobbler?" Grandma asked her.

Hattie thought for a minute. "At the pizza place, I think."

"Yes," Greta said. "I remember you saying you wanted steak and peach cobbler after . . ."

Suddenly, it hit us.

"What's going on?" Kodiak asked.

"Yeah," Roxy said. "What are you ladies thinking?"

I didn't want to be the one who said it, so I looked up at Grandma.

"Hattie has this strange thing where she smells things and then craves them," Grandma said slowly. She explained the koi pond and the trip to the leather store.

"What does that have to do with smelling me?"

Kodiak asked nervously. "You still don't think I had anything to do with Lou's murder, do you?"

"No," Grandma said, not wanting to break the news. "I think it was Madison."

Kodiak was shocked. "What? You guys are crazy. There's no way she would do that."

Grandma looked at Hattie again. "You mentioned peach cobbler for the first time after she walked away. You must have smelled some kind of body spray or perfume on her." Grandma glanced around the table at the rest of us. "When did Hattie talk about peach cobbler again?"

My mind was racing. I knew she had mentioned it several times, but I couldn't remember exactly when.

"After Lou was found dead in his dressing room," Virginia said, excitement rising in her voice. "Remember, she had walked in, and when she walked out, she said she wanted some."

"And in the barn," Greta added. "After she tried on Madison's scarf!"

Grandma looked at Kodiak. "And just now, after she hugged you," she said. "And you were with Madison tonight."

"That doesn't prove anything!" Kodiak yelled. "This is ridiculous!"

Archer looked at his friend. "Kodiak, did she know about the applesauce?"

"Everyone knew about the applesauce!" Kodiak defended.

Roxy reached out and touched his arm. "Did she sing for Lou? Was she in that theater?"

Kodiak was speechless. I could tell his mind was running through a thousand things at once. His mouth hung open, and he looked at each of us.

"She wouldn't do that," he finally said.

I felt bad for Kodiak. I wanted to somehow prove that we were wrong. "That still doesn't explain the horsehair," I said.

"It doesn't matter," Virginia said. "If we can prove that she played for Lou, and she was in the theater . . ."

"Wait a minute," Roxy said. "You said 'played for Lou.'"

"So?" Virginia said, confused.

"She plays the violin, right?" Roxy asked.

We all nodded.

"And what are violin bows made of?" She smiled, already knowing the answer.

The rest of us had no idea, except for Grandma.

"Horsehair," she answered.

"And remember," Greta said. "She told us after her show the other night that she was planning on moving on to bigger and better things."

Kodiak was still refusing to believe it.

"Call her up," Archer said. "Invite her to join us here tonight. We'll see if she'll talk."

"No!" Kodiak yelled. "I'm not going to put her in that position!"

Roxy touched his arm again to calm him down. "If

she's innocent, then we'll find out. If she isn't . . . wouldn't you want to know?"

Kodiak sat there defiant for a moment, then finally slumped over.

"Fine," he said, pulling out his phone. He was shaking as he sent her a text. He looked up. "She said she's excited, and she'll be right over."

Of course she's excited, I thought to myself. She thinks she's finally being invited into the inner circle, something she had apparently been trying to break into for weeks, if not months.

Nervous, quiet chatter took over our table until she finally arrived fifteen minutes later. She walked in all smiles, perfectly put together . . . and smelling like peaches. Kodiak noticed it immediately, and his smile fell. She kissed him and turned to look at the rest of us "My oh my, what a solemn group!"

She sat down, and her scent wafted across the table. I thought it was interesting that one could douse themselves with body spray, and it was okay, but if one did so with a spray that killed ninety-nine percent of bacteria, it was a faux pas.

We tried our best to act natural, but I thought we were all failing miserably. Archer took the lead on this one. "Welcome to the group, Madison. We've heard so much about you."

She beamed. "Thank you! That was so nice of y'all to invite me!"

"Did you hear how our preshow went tonight?" Archer asked her.

She looked up at Willie. "Was it a one-man show?"

Interesting, I thought. She knew that Billie had been arrested.

"Nah," Willie said, pulling Greta closer to him. "These ladies stepped up, and we put on our own variety show! It was a big hit."

"Really?" she asked, her voice cracking a bit.

"*Such* a big hit," Archer said, leaning forward, "that I decided to have them stay on and do it full time."

We all watched for her reaction, and we weren't disappointed. She tried to force a smile. "But you ladies don't have any experience. You're just here on vacation."

Archer pointed at Grandma Dean. "She used to be famous in Europe. I think she and her group will be quite a treasure to Branson."

"And unique," Roxy added. "There's no other group like them."

"Well," she said through gritted teeth that tried to resemble a smile. "Good for you, ladies. Welcome to Branson."

Kodiak couldn't take it anymore. He looked at Madison and took her hand. "Madison, did you play for Lou? Did he promise you a part in his group if you went out with him?"

Madison was shocked and instantly nervous. I

could tell she was about to clam up, and I think Roxy noticed it too.

"He did the same thing to me," Roxy said, her voice lowered. "I think he strung a lot of women along. It's not your fault."

Madison was surprised by this turn in the conversation. Her eyes flitted across the table, but it didn't look like she was actually looking at any of us. She was trying to think of her next move.

Roxy continued. "We think you might be one of his victims, and we wanted you to know that if you are, we're all here for you."

Madison's demeanor changed, and she took a breath. I still felt like she was guilty at this point, but she thought she was going to play us. And Roxy had done a great job of leading her right into our hands.

"It's true," she said, feigning sadness. "He promised that he could get me my own show."

"How long did you two see each other in secret?" Roxy asked.

"A month, maybe," Madison said. She looked up at Kodiak. "I'm so sorry. Please forgive me. I got sucked into his promises."

"It's not your fault," Roxy assured her. "I dated him for nearly two months. He would have me come to the theater to sing for him. Did he have you do the same?"

She nodded. "Sometimes on Archer's stage and sometimes in Lou's dressing room."

This was it. I could feel we were close to a confession, even if she said it by accident.

"When was the last time you played for him?" Roxy asked.

Madison closed her eyes, thinking. "A few days before he died." Her eyes suddenly filled with tears, and I was impressed with her acting skills.

"I . . . I played for him in the big theater, and he told me he was sure Willie and Billie would want me to play for them too. He kissed me and said it was finally my time. I left there feeling like it was actually going to happen. I got about halfway home, then I realized I had forgotten my bow, so I went back to get it."

She stopped talking, and Roxy handed her a tissue. Madison dabbed at her tears, then continued. "I knew I left it in his dressing room, and when I started down the hall, I could hear singing. At first, I was confused, but then I knew I had been played."

"Someone else was in there singing for him?" Roxy said, no doubt remembering when she had been in that same position herself.

Madison nodded. "I cracked open the door just as she finished, and Lou got up and kissed her and told her she had the voice of an angel. I was stunned. And then I saw who it was. That little nobody who sings out of that abandoned restaurant. I had seen her at the theater before. She works at the grocery store and delivers his applesauce every week . . ."

It felt like the wind was suddenly knocked out of me. Amy.

My head began to throb, and I looked up at Grandma, and she had the same look of alarm on her face. We had never completely ruled her out.

"How do you know she delivers the applesauce?" Grandma asked.

Madison sniffed. "I was there one morning when she dropped it off, and he told me. He said he can't swallow pills, so he puts it in his applesauce. Why?"

Grandma looked at Archer. "Didn't the police check to see where he got the applesauce?"

"I don't know," Archer said, concerned. "But I'll find out." He pulled out his phone and started to text someone.

Madison was crying, and Kodiak put his arm around her. He gave us all a look that said he wasn't happy with us. And we deserved it. I felt terrible, and judging from the looks on everyone else's faces, they did too.

"Come on," Kodiak said. "I'll walk you out to your car."

We said goodbye to Madison and watched as she and Kodiak walked out the door.

Archer got a call, and he walked toward the bathroom to take it. The rest of us sat at the table, feeling guilty.

"Well, that didn't go like you planned," Casius said. He had been so quiet I had forgotten he was there.

"I feel terrible," Greta said. "We blamed that poor girl and really, she was innocent."

"And Amy," I said shaking my head in disbelief. "Here we thought she was so sweet, and she was the murderer all along."

"Her meeting with Lou must have upset her more than she let on," Virginia said.

"Or," Roxy added, "she realized she was just being led on like the rest of us and decided to pay him back."

"Whatever the reason," Grandma Dean said, "Archer will tell his police friend, and they'll sort it all out."

Archer came back to the table and slammed his phone down. That took all of us by surprise. "Guess what my buddy at the station said."

We looked at him, waiting for him to tell us.

"They *did* question Amy. She admitted to meeting him at the grocery store one day, and he told her about his medication. She started delivering him a case every week."

"So, it was her, then," Greta said sadly.

"He also said they think the applesauce was contaminated inside the mini fridge. They found traces of antifreeze at the bottom like it had been spilled. Most likely the killer snuck in and added it to whatever was in his fridge at the time—his applesauce, his drinks . . . It was a sloppy job, so whoever did it was trying to be quick."

"Wait a minute," Virginia said. "Amy told us she performed once for him, and it was on Archer's stage.

But Madison just said she was in Lou's dressing room."

"Is Amy a suspect?" Grandma asked Archer.

He shook his head. "They cleared her on day one."

"Does that mean that Madison is guilty after all?" I asked.

"What if," Roxy said, "Madison came back just like she said she did, and she saw Amy on the stage. And she decided then to put an end to Lou. She ran out to her car, grabbed antifreeze, and took it to his dressing room. After she put it in his applesauce, and who knows what else, she hid it in Billie's dressing room so she wouldn't be caught walking out with it."

Casius laughed.

"What's so funny?" I asked.

"Madison just played us all like a fiddle."

22

"WHERE'S KODIAK?" I asked a few minutes later. "Shouldn't he have been back in here by now?"

Grandma stood up, a worried look on her face. "Let's go check on him."

We all went outside and looked around. There were a handful of vehicles in the parking lot, and one of them was Kodiak's truck. Hattie walked ahead of us as we made our way toward it.

All of a sudden Hattie shrieked. "He's dead! She got him!"

We ran up to the truck and saw Kodiak slumped over the steering wheel. Hattie flung the door open and jumped in, climbing on Kodiak and pulling his head back. She immediately started giving him mouth-to-mouth. It took me a second to realize he was struggling to get away.

"Hattie!" I yelled. "Let him go! He's not dead!"

Finally, Kodiak was able to pull her off of him. His eyes were bulging. "What the heck is going on?" he demanded.

Hattie smiled. "You were dead, and I brought you back to life."

"Dead?" Kodiak yelled. "I wasn't dead! I was just sitting here thinking. And then you jumped in and nearly gave me a heart attack!

Hattie's smile broadened. "It's nice to know I can still stop a man's heart."

"What are you doing out here?" I asked Kodiak. "Is everything okay?"

The look on Kodiak's face changed from fear to sadness. "She broke up with me. She said she couldn't be with a man who would just sit there while someone accused her of murder."

"Kodiak," I said gently. "We still think she's guilty."

He looked at all of us—old friends and new. "I know," he said slowly. "I didn't want to believe it at first. But I think you guys are right."

"Where did she go?" Archer asked. "Is she headed home?"

Kodiak shrugged. "She was upset when she left, so I offered to take her home, but she said she had to pick something up at the grocery store first."

"The grocery store?" Grandma asked, alarmed. "You don't think she would hurt Amy, do you?"

Virginia reached in her purse and pulled out her

keys. "Nikki, you and Kodiak run by the store to see if Amy's there. Kodiak, give us Madison's address, and we'll run by her house and see what she's up to."

Kodiak rattled off an address as Casius and I climbed in his truck. The grannies, along with Willie and Roxy and Archer, crammed themselves into Virginia's SUV. It could seat eight, but it was still going to be a tight fit with everyone.

I told Kodiak what grocery store I thought Amy worked at, and we made our way over there in silence. I could tell that Kodiak was nervous, and Casius, well, he was unusually quiet.

We pulled up in front of the grocery store, and Kodiak put the truck in park. "Now what?"

"I'll go in and see if Amy is working," I said, opening the door. "I'll be right back."

The automatic doors of the grocery store slid open, revealing a bright and cheerful store. It was late at night, but you'd never know it walking around in there. I almost felt like I needed to shield my eyes, the store was so bright. I saw a manager helping out a cashier, and I stood by the bagger until the manager turned to walk away.

"Excuse me," I said to her. "Is Amy Walters here?"

The manager's face fell. "She was until a few minutes ago. Someone came in and told her she had a family emergency, and she had to leave."

My heart dropped. "She didn't leave with her, did

she?" I asked, silently praying the manager would say no.

"I think so," the manager answered. "They walked out together."

"Crap!" I yelled, running toward the door. I pulled out my cell phone and called Grandma. "Madison was already here. Amy left with her a few minutes ago."

"We're almost to Madison's house," Grandma said. "Archer is calling his police friend right now, but at this rate, we'll get there before they do."

"I'll head your way," I promised.

As I was running to the truck, I saw Casius hanging out the window, waving wildly. "Hurry up!" he yelled at me. "We just saw Madison leave the parking lot, and there was a woman in the front seat!"

I ran even faster and climbed in. Kodiak sped out of the parking lot and pulled up at a red light.

He banged on the steering wheel. "We're going to lose her!"

Even though it was late, there were still several cars out on the road. Kodiak pointed to red taillights that were nearly a block away and getting further. "That's her up there."

The light turned green, and Kodiak floored it. The taillights were a few blocks ahead of us at this point. She turned right, and when Kodiak finally caught up to the street to turn right himself, there was no sign of her car.

"Where did she go?" Casius asked, looking around.

We were on a straight country road. Even with her being far ahead of us, we still should've been able to see her taillights. But we were the only people on the road.

Grandma sent me a text letting me know Madison wasn't at her house, and I told her what was going on. When I told her where we were, she said that wasn't too far from Madison's house, and they would head our way.

"Kill the lights," I ordered Kodiak.

"Nikki, it's too dark out here. I won't be able to see anything."

I gave him a hard stare and he huffed. "Fine." He flicked off the lights, and we rolled our windows down, hoping to hear or see something as we slowly made our way down the road.

My phone rang, and I nearly peed on myself from fright.

"Geez Nikki," Casius said, punching me in the arm. "Turn off your ringer. We're supposed to be in stealth mode."

I answered the phone in a whisper, though I probably didn't need to.

"Greta just looked up Amy's address, and it's close to where you are," Grandma said urgently. "I think that's where they're headed. I'm going to text you the address. You guys head there. We're on our way. Archer's on the phone now with his cop buddy."

I hung up and relayed the message to the guys.

Grandma's text came through, and I put the address in the GPS on my phone.

"It's not even a mile from here!"

Casius took my phone. "Kodiak, look for a street up ahead and take a right. Keep your lights off."

"I'm not an owl!" Kodiak barked. "It's nearly impossible to see out here."

We drove along, all looking for the road. The trees on either side of the road made it even more difficult to see.

"There!" Casius pointed out. "You just missed it!"

Kodiak put the truck in reverse a few feet and turned onto the road.

"She lives down here," Casius said, still holding my phone.

He flipped the phone over so it hid the light from the screen. As we made our way down the road, it felt like my heart was in my throat. Casius must have felt nervous too, because he grabbed my hand.

Before I could even see Amy's house, I could hear shouting.

"Pull over," I said to Kodiak. "We'll walk the rest of the way so she doesn't see us coming."

"Shouldn't we wait for the police?" Casius asked, alarmed.

"We never wait for the police," I said, taking off my seat belt.

Kodiak and Casius both looked over at me, surprised.

"You've done this before?" Casius asked.

"It's kind of our thing. I'll explain later."

Kodiak pulled the truck to the side of the road and turned it off. I helped Casius out of the truck, and we quietly made our way toward the shouting. It was definitely Madison and Amy, though I couldn't understand what they were saying. I wished the grannies were here. They always took charge in these situations. I could feel the adrenaline burning in my veins. My fight or flight was kicking in, and I was leaning toward flight.

But then I thought about all the times the grannies and I had been in these situations, and did they back down? No. They ran full force into danger. They never let fear get in their way. I knew that if I didn't act fast, Amy would be Madison's next victim.

We were now standing at the end of Amy's driveway. Her porch light was on, illuminating her yard where she and Madison stood arguing. Madison had her back to me, and she was blocking my view of Amy. But I could sense the danger. I knew I needed to act fast. And then I heard the word that made my heart stop. Gun.

I reached over and grabbed a crutch from under Casius' arm and charged toward the women. I heard Casius falter behind me, and I hoped that Kodiak was able to grab him before he hit the ground.

I ran through the yard and raised the crutch just as I approached them. I swung it through the air, and it collided with Madison's shoulder. I had been aiming for her head, but it still did the trick, knocking her over. She laid on the ground shrieking in pain. I looked up at Amy to see if she was okay, and I suddenly froze. She was the one who had the gun, and now it was pointed directly at me.

"Amy?" I finally squeaked out in disbelief. "What are you doing?"

She scowled at me. "Why can't you people just go on a vacation like everyone else? Go to a show, eat at new restaurants, buy souvenirs? No, you have to go poking around where you don't belong."

I looked at Madison, who was still on the ground, holding her shoulder.

"So, which one of you killed Lou?" I asked, completely confused.

"Amy did it!" Madison yelled. "Amy killed him!"

"I did not!" Amy shouted. "You killed him! All I did was distract him that night so you could sneak into his dressing room with the antifreeze!"

"You were in on it together?" I asked, shocked. "Amy, you were so nice. Why would you do something like that?"

She sniffed, and tears welled up in her eyes. "Madison told me that if I helped her move up, she would help me move up. I thought we were just going to make him sick. I didn't know he was actually going to die."

"Shut up!" Madison yelled from the ground. "Don't tell her anything else!"

I never took my eyes off of Amy or the gun. "Amy, let's put the gun down. You can explain to the police what happened. If you tell them the whole truth, I'm sure they will give you a smaller sentence."

"No," Amy said firmly. "I'm not going down for this. I'm going to shoot Madison and tell the police that she came here to kill me, and I shot her in self-defense." She looked at me and shook her head sadly. "I just have to figure out what to do with you."

I was thankful she didn't realize I wasn't alone, though I didn't think Kodiak or Casius would be much help to me.

"I don't understand any of this, Amy," I said, trying to stall and hoping and praying the grannies or the police would show up any minute.

"What is left to understand?" she asked. "Madison wanted Lou's job, and she said she would talk to the Seven Sven about hiring me to replace her. Lou made it easy. When he invited me to sing for him, I told Madison, and she came up with the plan. As soon as my bandmates left, I sent her a text. She was waiting nearby . . ."

"I said shut up!" Madison screamed. She struggled to stand, still not taking her hand off her shoulder.

"When did this happen?" I asked. "When did she put the antifreeze in his applesauce?"

"The same day I met you for the first time. Madison

177

and I were at the pizza restaurant so we would have an alibi."

That's why Madison was there handing out flyers, even though she already worked for a successful show.

"That's enough!" Madison yelled, now on her feet. She reached for the crutch that was still in my hand, but I held it firmly. She tried to jerk it away from me, but I tried to pull it away from her. Soon we were in a tug of war over the crutch, and it seemed to push Amy over the edge.

"I can't take this anymore!" Amy yelled. She pointed the gun at Madison. "This is all your fault! We're in this mess because of you!"

She had enough panic in her voice that I knew this was it—she was going to pull the trigger.

I tried to pull the crutch out of Madison's hand one last time, hoping I could get control of it and knock the gun out of Amy's hand. I'm guessing Madison had the same idea, because just as I pulled, she pulled too. Neither of us was letting go. I closed my eyes. I couldn't watch it happen. I couldn't watch Madison get shot right there in front of me.

I squeezed my eyes tight and waited for the blast of the gun. But instead, I heard a high-pitched sound like something whizzed in front of me. I heard a cry and opened my eyes to see Amy staring blankly in front of her. Her eyes were wide, and her mouth hung open, but she stood perfectly still for just a moment, then she collapsed in a heap on the ground.

What had happened? Then I saw it. A dart was sticking out of Amy's arm. Before I could react, I heard the whizzing sound again, and this time Madison let out a cry as she grabbed her arm. She swayed, and I could see her eyes struggling to stay focused. She fell to her knees then slumped over.

I looked over toward where the darts had come from, and I saw Casius give Kodiak a high five. "Tranquilizer darts!" Kodiak shouted to me. "I always keep some with me because of the animals."

I heard sirens, and soon, the yard was lit up with red-and-blue lights. The grannies were right behind them.

While I talked to the police, I could see Kodiak and Casius filling the grannies in on everything they missed.

I walked up to them as Kodiak finished his story. "What kind of tranquilizer did you use?" Hattie asked him. "Mine doesn't work nearly that fast on humans. It takes several minutes for it to kick in."

Kodiak beamed proudly. "Well, you have to mix . . ."

"Don't answer that," Grandma warned Kodiak. "Hattie doesn't need to know the answer. She's dangerous enough as she is."

I handed Casius his crutch. "These metal crutches are great. I'm pretty sure a wooden one wouldn't have held up as well."

Casius looked at me and his eyes narrowed. "Who exactly *are* you?"

I couldn't help but laugh. "A little mystery is fun. You of all people should know that."

When I didn't offer him any more information, he laughed and shook his head. "All right then. A woman of mystery. I like that."

23

THE NEXT MORNING, Grandma and I packed our suitcases.

"Are you sure you don't want to stay another day?" I asked. "We didn't even have a chance to relax."

"I'm sure," Grandma said. "I'm ready to go to Lou's memorial and then head home."

I stopped packing and looked up at her. "And stop by Thomas' house on the way out of town, right?"

She sighed. "Yes, we'll stop by his house on the way out."

Grandma had been putting off that visit since we got here, even though it was the whole purpose of making this road trip. Even if she decided not to see him, I didn't think the other grannies would let her leave without stopping by his house.

We met the other grannies in the lobby, and we all turned in our keys. We said goodbye to Paulette, and

Hattie ran outside to get one more look at the koi pond. Minutes later, we were pulling out of the hotel parking lot, leaving the charming little place behind us.

We grabbed a quick lunch and pulled up at the theater thirty minutes before the memorial was about to start. We parked next to Roxy's car and made our way inside.

Archer was standing at the door when we walked in, and he gave Grandma a big hug. I noticed how tightly Grandma held on when she hugged him back. They were already preparing to say their goodbyes.

Willie walked over and threw his arm around Greta, and Virginia's face fell. I was just about to ask about Billie when he walked through the door. Virginia squealed like a high schooler and threw her arms around him. He was clearly happy to see her too.

Willie gave his brother a hug. "I see you got cleaned up after you left the station this morning."

Billie laughed. "I never needed a shower so bad in my life!"

Archer clapped Billie on the back. "I'm glad you're back. And I heard that all the charges against you have been dropped."

Casius walked up to the door, and I held it open for him while he hobbled in on his crutches.

"I'm so sick of these things," he said. "Do you know how difficult it is to perform with crutches?"

"I can't believe you're still performing," I said to him.

He just smiled. "The show must go on."

Archer took Grandma's hand. "Come on. Let's go to my dressing room and practice our duet."

As they walked away, Hattie and Irene decided they wanted to practice too. Billie said they could use his dressing room since it was no longer a crime scene. He walked away with them, and Greta and Virginia followed behind. That left Casius and me standing in the lobby of the theater.

"Have you talked to Kodiak today?" I asked him.

He shook his head. "No, I left a message and then sent him a text. I'm sure he'll be here, but I don't know what kind of shape he'll be in."

I felt so bad for him. He really liked Madison.

"So, are you actually headed home today?" he asked me.

I sighed. "Yeah, I wish we could stay another day."

"I do too," he admitted.

I looked at him, the mysterious magician with dark eyes and an even darker persona. But all I really saw was a kindhearted, misunderstood man.

"What would another day even do for us?" I asked.

He shrugged. "Just another day to put off saying goodbye, I suppose." He nudged me and smiled. "It was nice having you around."

"Thanks." I laughed. "It was nice to be around."

He was quiet for a minute. "You know, if you ever figure out who you are and what you want, and if you ever think it might be some dusky and risky fellow, you know how to get ahold of me."

Now I really laughed. "Well, no one is as dusky and risky as you are."

We were having the memorial service in the same room where Willie, Billie, and Lou always performed because Archer said it felt more personal than his big stage and huge auditorium. Casius and I took our seats and listened to Roxy Rococo practicing her version of "Amazing Grace." I had never heard it sung with a level of edginess to it, but for some reason, it felt very fitting.

Kodiak startled us when he came up and sat down next to Casius.

"You okay, man?" Casius whispered to him.

Kodiak shrugged. He didn't look okay.

Casius reached in his pocket and pulled out a card. "Here," he said, handing it to Kodiak. "In case you ever need it."

"Is this your number?" Kodiak smiled. "You're finally giving it to me?" He waved it in the air to show me. "I can actually call the legend himself instead of having to call his assistant to see if he needs a ride somewhere."

"Abuse that privilege, and I'll change my number," Casius laughed.

Seeing them talking and teasing each other made my heart happy. Kodiak was going to be okay. And Casius was too. Even though they had known each other for a long time, they were finally becoming friends.

Greta and Virginia came and sat next to me, and soon, others were filing in. I recognized the Seven Sven as the family took their seats behind us.

Hattie and Irene came out and asked us to save some seats for their Mennonite friends. "They're really excited about seeing us perform," Hattie said. "Plus, they feel like they're getting a free concert. They're a thrifty bunch."

Irene looked at Virginia, who was sitting at the end. She motioned at the empty seats next to her. "Can they sit by you? Will you make them feel welcomed?"

"Of course," Virginia said. "We're excited to meet them."

When Hattie and Irene walked away, Virginia turned toward us. "Can you believe those two? What a change in just a few days. I wonder how long it will last?"

Greta laughed. "I bet you we don't even make it out of Missouri."

We all made small talk for the next several minutes as more people came in and took their seats. The Mennonites came in, and Virginia and I jumped up to bring them up to our row. Samuel and Amos, along with Samuel's daughter and son-in-law and their oldest daughter, Emily. As soon as she saw me, she blushed, probably remembering the last time we saw each other. Maybe I would have to explain to her that I didn't normally parade around in leopard outfits, or maybe it would just be better to let that go.

The lights flickered to let everyone know that the memorial service would soon be starting. Archer Nash took the stage, and the crowd went silent. He started the service with a prayer, and then Grandma walked on the stage and sat on a stool in front of a microphone. "We're going to sing one of Lou's favorites. As some of you know, Lou was a fan of James Taylor. If you know the words to 'You Can Close Your Eyes,' you can sing along with us."

Archer started to play the guitar, and Grandma sang. I had never heard the song before, but the many performers in the room couldn't help themselves. None of them upstaged Grandma, but they sang along quietly.

Roxy Rococo came out and did her version of "Amazing Grace" and "Somewhere Over the Rainbow."

Then it was Hattie and Irene's turn. Just like they had the night before, they sang beautifully. I even saw Samuel wipe a tear from his eyes when they sang "How Great Thou Art."

Then Archer took the stage again. "Lou performed on this stage for many years and he brought a lot of laughter and happiness to people. But he was human, and he made a lot of mistakes. It's a shame that he isn't here to rectify what he has done, but I want to apologize to any of you he may have hurt or misled."

I was surprised by his apology, but I knew that it

meant something to Roxy and maybe to anyone else Lou had scammed.

"But we're not here today to focus on that," Archer said. "We're here to give Lou a Branson sendoff he would've been proud of. So, let's sing so loud that the ole coot can hear us no matter where he is."

Willie and Billie took the stage and led us all through a singalong. We clapped and sang and stomped. It was the most joyful memorial I had ever been to. And when it was over, I was exhausted. I felt like I had just done an hour's worth of cardio . . . which I probably had.

"You guys were amazing," I said to Willie and Billie when we were back in the lobby, once it was over.

"Thanks," Billie said. "Lou made some bad choices, but we loved him like a brother."

Hattie and Irene said goodbye to their Mennonite friends, and I watched as Greta and Virginia started their goodbyes with Willie and Billie. Grandma and Archer were talking in the corner, and I stood here alone.

Casius and Kodiak came up next to me.

"I don't like goodbyes," Casius said. "I'm much better with disappearing acts."

I hugged him. "No more slipping in dog pee. You take care of yourself."

He laughed but looked a little hurt. "You act like you're never going to see me again."

Kodiak put his arms around me and hugged me

187

tight. "You and those grandmas are crazy enough to make it work out here. You sure you don't want to give it a try?"

"I'm sure," I said, still hugging him. "It's time to go back."

He let go of me. "Well, I hope you keep in touch. I think Casius especially would like that, wouldn't you, Cas . . ." Kodiak turned around, but Casius was gone. We looked around the near empty lobby, but he wasn't there.

Casius never even said goodbye. He really was good at disappearing acts.

2 4

WE DROVE in silence along the twisty country road. The only noise was the occasional directions from Virginia's GPS.

I looked out the window, up at the cloudy sky, as giant raindrops began to fall. Soon, the windshield wipers were swiping rapidly, and it seemed to add to the anxiety in the car.

Not only did the grannies each say goodbye to people who had become special to them, but Grandma was about to come face-to-face with someone special from her past.

It felt like we had been driving forever when we finally pulled onto a long driveway that led up to a house sitting in a clearing of trees. The rain had let up enough that no one grabbed an umbrella as we walked up to the front porch.

"You're sure this is the address?" Grandma asked. "I expected something more . . . opulent."

The outside of the country house was neatly kept, with plants on the front porch and hanging baskets of impatiens swaying from the afternoon storm.

"It's the address we found online," Virginia said. "Would you like to ring the doorbell or should I?"

Virginia wasn't giving Grandma a chance to back out.

"I'll do it," Grandma said, stepping forward.

She hit the button, and we could hear it ring throughout the house. A tiny dog started barking, and we heard a woman shush it from just beyond the door.

My heart was pounding. I couldn't even imagine what Grandma's must be doing.

A woman who looked to be in her late forties or early fifties opened the door, holding a fluffy black dog. She smiled but seemed a little confused as she greeted us.

Grandma cleared her throat. "Is Thomas here?" she asked.

The woman's smile dropped. "I'm sorry to have to tell you this, but he passed three months ago. Were you friends of his?"

We stood there stunned, not able to answer her question.

Then she looked at Grandma and squinted a bit. "You're not Geraldine, are you?"

"I am," Grandma answered, her voice cracking. "How did you know?"

The woman smiled again and invited us in. The home was bright and cheerful and looked immaculately clean. She pointed to the living room furniture, which was well worn with crocheted pillows tucked in the corners. Grandma, Greta, and I sat on the couch while Hattie and Irene took the love seat. The woman went to the kitchen and brought out two chairs from the table—one for her and one for Virginia.

The woman sat down. "I can't believe you're here. Mother would've flipped out if she had gotten to meet you."

"Mother?" I asked.

"Oh yes," the woman said. "She was a big fan."

I think we were all a little confused.

She had put her dog down to get the chairs, and now the little thing wanted back up in her lap. She scooped it up. "This is my dog Beanie, and my name is Laura. I'm Thomas' and Eva's youngest daughter."

We went around the room and introduced ourselves.

"How would your mother know my grandmother?" I asked her.

"Oh!" she said, popping up from her chair. "I'll show you."

She disappeared through a door and came back with a photo album. She handed it to Grandma and took her seat back on the wooden kitchen chair. Beanie squirmed to get comfortable in her lap again.

"Go ahead," she smiled. "Open it."

As Grandma did, Laura went on to explain its contents. "Mother knew all about you and Daddy. She was always kind of obsessed." She laughed. "Not in some creepy way, but she was fascinated with your life and how close she came to knowing a celebrity. She kept up with your career and kept this scrapbook."

Grandma flipped through pictures of her and newspaper articles.

"It used to drive Daddy nuts." Laura chuckled. "But it was like one of Mother's hobbies."

Grandma finished flipping through the book, then passed it to us so we could look through it.

"I don't understand any of this," Grandma admitted. "Did she know I was married to him for a short while?"

"Yes," Laura said sadly. "And I'm so sorry for how you were treated. Mother always said you paved the way for her. Maybe that's why she admired you so much."

"Did he know they had a daughter together?" I asked her, and the look on her face was a dead giveaway that she didn't.

"I had no idea," she said. "Are you any relation to her?"

"She's my mother."

Laura jumped from her seat again, and poor Beanie yelped in surprise. Laura ran over to me and pulled me to my feet. "That means we're related! I would be your aunt!" She threw her arms around me and held me tight.

Up until that moment, I was only thinking about how this affected Grandma Dean. I hadn't thought about me potentially meeting family for the first time.

She let go. "I'm so sorry. I get a little over excited sometimes." She looked us over. "I still can't believe that you're here."

She walked over to an end table and pulled out more photo albums, and instead of taking a seat on her chair, she sat on the coffee table facing us. She opened her book. "Here are Mother and Daddy on their wedding day."

We looked at the date. "That was just a year after he was forced to leave me," Grandma said sadly. "I was still thinking I could win him back. I had no idea he was already remarried."

I felt so bad for Grandma. This visit wasn't giving her the kind of closure I had hoped it would.

"He was devastated, you know," Laura told her. "Mother told me about how they met. She worked at a little restaurant in town, and he would come in every day and sit in the corner and just stare outside. Finally, one day Mother got up enough courage to talk to him about why he was there, and he told her he hoped that one day you'd walk by."

Grandma's eyes filled with tears.

"I don't know if it makes you feel any better, but I

don't think he ever stopped caring about you. Even though he would complain every time Mother pulled out that scrapbook and added to it, he always had to look at the picture or article and see what she was putting in there."

"If he cared so much, then why didn't he come after me?" Grandma asked.

Laura sighed. "I think he looked at your moving to Europe as you moving on. He didn't want to get in the way of your happiness."

"I don't understand something," Greta chimed in. "I don't mean to upset you or anything, but how is it that Geraldine wasn't good enough for your father, and yet your mother was? It wasn't like she was royalty. She worked at a restaurant."

Thankfully, Laura didn't act like the question upset her at all. "Well," she began, "after you left the country, Daddy and his mother had a big falling out. And when he decided to marry my mother, his own mother gave him an ultimatum—leave her or give up any right to the family business. He decided not to let his mother live his life for him anymore, so, he gave it all up."

"Really?" Grandma asked. "He actually walked away from her and the money?"

"Yep," Laura answered. "He moved down here to be closer to my mother's family, and he opened up his own little shoe store. It did pretty well, enough to take care of all of us. My parents owned their own home and shared one car. We lived a pretty simple life, but I have so many wonderful memories."

"What ever happened to Thomas' mother?" I asked. "Did she ever apologize or come around and try to make things right?"

Laura shook her head. "Never. I never even met her. She died about ten years ago, and Daddy had been completely cut out of her will, just like she promised."

"What a horrible woman," Virginia said, and Laura agreed.

"So, what happened to Thomas?" Grandma asked sadly. "How did he die?"

"Heart attack," Laura said. "Mother passed away last year, and he was just never the same. My brothers and I knew it wouldn't be long until he joined her. They were always inseparable."

"Well," Grandma said to her, "it looks like they lived a good life together."

"They did," Laura said, standing and taking her place back in her chair. "But I think Mother was always a little jealous of yours."

"Mine?" Grandma asked.

"Oh yes," Laura said. "Daddy never went anywhere. If he took a vacation day, he spent it in the yard. Would you believe we never went on a single trip during my childhood? I think Mother lived through you and your adventures. She would always beg him to take her somewhere, but he would say 'I spent half my life trying to find home. Why would I leave it?'"

The room was quiet except for the sound of Beanie snoring from her little dog bed in the corner.

"Would you like to know where he's buried?" Laura asked. "I can write down the address."

Grandma didn't answer right away, but Virginia said that yes, we would like it.

We sat and visited for a few more minutes, and then we said our goodbyes. As we were leaving, Laura slipped me a picture of herself.

"You can give this to your mother," she told me. "I'd love to meet her sometime, if she's up for it."

I thanked her and followed the grannies out to the vehicle. This had definitely not been the visit any of us expected.

Without saying a word, Virginia typed in the address Laura had given her, and we sat in silence again as we took the winding roads through the country. The sun was out now, and the world seemed completely oblivious to the pain in Grandma's heart. But I knew it was there.

We pulled into the parking lot of an old church and could see the cemetery behind it.

"Would you like us to come with you?" Irene asked.

Grandma shook her head no.

She got out of the SUV, and her heels crunched along on the gravel as she made her way across the parking lot. She went row by row until she suddenly stopped. She dropped to her knees, and I think all of us were in tears watching her. She was finally able to say goodbye.

She stayed out there for a long time, and after a while, the grannies and I started to pull out our phones. I was in the middle of a word game when the door opened, and Grandma was standing there, her pant legs wet from the grass, and her eyes swollen and red, but still, she was smiling.

"Let's go," she said, climbing in.

Virginia turned around and looked at her. "You okay?"

"I can honestly say I *am* okay," Grandma answered. "I got a glimpse today of what my life would've looked like had things worked out the way I had originally hoped. And I know I would've been happy for a while, but not for long. Things happen for a reason, and Thomas married someone that was better suited for him. I have loved living my life—the adventure, the grandeur, everything that was in that scrapbook his wife kept. That's me. That's the life I'm thankful I got to live."

"Well," Virginia said to us, "are we heading home?"

"Yes," we all said, suddenly emotionally and physically exhausted from our trip.

"Wait a minute!" Irene said. "We never made it to the Butterfly Palace, and Hattie didn't get her peach cobbler!"

"Ugh," Hattie grunted. "I don't want that anymore. I want a big ole slice of key lime pie. Let's go home."

"And as far as the Butterfly Palace," Grandma said, smiling, "now we'll have another reason to come back." She pulled out her phone, and I could see she was texting Archer.

I was happy for Grandma Dean. Not only did she get the closure she wanted, she was also opening a door she had sealed shut long ago. And I had a feeling we'd be seeing Archer Nash again.

Thank You

Thanks for reading *Road Trip*. I have a lot of fun writing the Glock Grannies books and I hope you have fun reading them!

There are many more adventures coming so keep an eye out on Amazon for the next Glock Granny's novel.

In the mean time, be sure to check out all my books on Amazon.

If you could take a minute, it would be really nice if you left a review for me. That really helps me tell other readers about the book.

Lastly, if you would like to know about future cozy mysteries by me and the other authors at Fairfield Publishing, make sure to sign up for our Cozy Mystery Newsletter. We will send you our FREE Cozy Mystery Starter Library just for signing up. All the details are on the next page.

FAIRFIELD COZY MYSTERY NEWSLETTER

Make sure you sign up for the Fairfield Cozy Mystery Newsletter so you can keep up with our latest releases. When you sign up, **we will send you our FREE Cozy Mystery Starter Library!**

FairfieldPublishing.com/cozy-newsletter/

Made in the USA
Monee, IL
02 July 2021